S IS FOR SECRET BABY

ANNIE J. ROSE

Photography: Wander Aguiar

CHAPTER 1

WES

I frowned at the number of emails in my inbox. Jesus. It was always the same, but it always seemed to catch me off guard: take just one afternoon off, and the next day you somehow had two thousand emails to weed through. This was at a relatively small business, too. I could only imagine what it was like if you worked for one of those crazy city-based companies.

Granted, if I worked for one of those companies, I doubted I would even have the luxury of taking even half an hour off, let alone half a day.

Before I could really get into answering my emails, there was a knock at the door. I looked up to see my assistant Beth standing there. She had a file in her hand and a disgruntled look on her face. "The new girl is in the lobby," she informed me in a clipped tone. I raised an eyebrow at her as she tossed the folder on my desk and crossed her arms.

I suppressed a sigh. It was clear that Beth already didn't like the new hire. Not that it was really any of her business. I mean, okay, she was probably worried that as my assistant, she would need to pick up any slack that the new hire couldn't keep up with. She should have known by now that wasn't the way I ran the company, though. Besides, it was inappropriate for her to be so vocal about her dislike for the new woman, especially since she barely knew the girl.

It was on the tip of my tongue to chastise Beth, but I knew that wouldn't go over well. See, she used to be the owner's assistant, but since George went into semi-retirement, I had inherited her. She wasn't the person I would necessarily have chosen as an assistant, but that was purely from a personality standpoint. At the end of the day, she knew what she was doing, and she was loyal to the company. That meant a lot.

That said, she took liberties I typically wouldn't permit. There were certain behaviors I wanted to nip in the bud before too long. Still, now might not be the best time, with the new girl waiting down in the lobby.

"What's your impression of her?" I asked Beth mildly. Maybe if she talked about it and I was able to shut down any ridiculous preconceptions she had, she would take it easy on the new girl. That was probably the best I could do for now.

Beth rolled her eyes, further cementing my impression that there was something about the new girl she didn't approve of. "She's some big-city businesswoman who clearly thinks she's too good to be out here in the sticks," she said, her tone dripping with disdain.

I tried not to wince, knowing that would only give Beth more reason to side against the new girl. No, I didn't want to validate her impressions if I could help it. Even if I honestly didn't have the time to deal with someone who thought they were too good for this place.

Besides, I wouldn't have ended up as CEO of the biggest company in my hometown if I wasn't damned proud of being from there. We might be a small town in Nebraska, overlooked by most of the rest of the world, but we had made a name in the business world. Not to mention that people here were friendly, and life moved at a pace I was comfortable with. I wouldn't trade it for anywhere else.

So no, I didn't particularly like the idea of someone coming in here who thought they could do better than this. I didn't mention that to Beth, though. Instead, in an equally mild tone, I just said, "I'm sure she'll find a way to fit in eventually."

Beth's face darkened, and I could tell that when she opened her mouth again, it would be to say something even more unkind about the new hire. Suddenly, I felt as though I'd heard enough. "You're more than welcome to express your opinion, especially in a general form," I said sternly, "but I won't tolerate rudeness or unprofessionalism in this company."

Beth's mouth tightened into a thin line, but she nodded. "All right," she said coolly.

"Please show her in," I instructed, turning to the file she had carelessly tossed on my desk. I hadn't had a chance yet to look up any information about the new innovations manager that George had hired just before he turned the reins of the company over to me. Things had been crazy during the transition period, and anyway, I trusted George had picked someone well-suited to the position.

I had worked with this company ever since I graduated from business school, and that was quite long enough to know that George knew what he was doing. He and I didn't always see eye to eye, and especially not where personnel was concerned, but he would have hired someone who was at least competent.

I flipped open the file and stared down at the name that was in bold at the top of the résumé. My mouth dropped open.

Rian James. No way.

Surely it had to be another person. But then again, how many girls were there named "Rian"? To have the same last name as well... No way, though. She wouldn't come back to Nebraska. Would she?

I looked up as the door opened again. Beth walked in with a fake smile plastered on her face. My eyes slid past her to the woman following her, however. There was no doubt about it: she was absolutely the same Rian James I remembered.

The same Rian James who was my nemesis in business school. The same Rian James that I fell half in love with until she snagged my dream internship out from under me.

Our eyes locked, and I felt a surge of electricity go through me. She was even more beautiful than she was seven years ago. And it was clear that she recognized me, too. An unreadable emotion flitted across her face, but she quickly controlled her expression. It left me wondering what she was thinking. Not that I could ask.

"Wes, this is Rian James. Rian, Wes—the CEO of GBC," Beth said, and it was all I could do to keep from blurting out the fact that we already knew one another. Oh, we knew one another *very* well. My mind flashed back to that night, her silky skin spread out beneath me on the sheets, and I tried very hard to push those images away and focus on the present.

Fortunately, Beth didn't seem to want to stick around. She slipped out of the office, leaving me alone with Rian. I wasn't sure whether that was a good thing or not.

"Rian," I said, wondering if my voice sounded as choked to her as it did to myself. "Seeing you again is an... unexpected surprise."

Rian frowned. "I thought I'd be meeting with George Austin," she said.

"George recently handed over the reins of the company to

me when he went into semi-retirement," I informed her. "I will be your direct supervisor."

A look of panic appeared in Rian's eyes, and she quickly looked away. I couldn't help but feel unsettled. Was that a normal reaction? I didn't know why she would look *panicked*, though. Unhappy, maybe. Concerned, perhaps. But panicked?

Back in college, we were both at the top of our business school class. It seemed like we went head-to-head for everything in our projects, competing for the best internships and chances at graduate programs. It all came to a point at the very end of our time at school, with one final project. According to our advisor, my project was the more polished of the two of ours, but somehow, she had still managed to edge me out of the internship of my dreams.

The real kicker of it all? I only found out that she had landed the internship after she left town for New York City. After she had broken my heart.

That one night was all that we had together, but it was still etched there in my brain. I could remember it as well as any other memory I had, and then some. Every detail, every feeling, and every taste lingered in my head.

I tried not to think about that, though. Especially not now. I had to keep it together and be professional. I was her boss now, and employee relationships were strictly not allowed. She was completely off-limits.

That was a good thing, anyway. I hadn't forgiven her yet for disappearing like she had, and I wasn't sure that I wanted to. Even if she had been available, I knew better than to start anything with her anytime soon.

To distract myself, I flipped through her résumé, humming in interest as I saw the various positions she had worked in the years since I had last seen her. I had to admit it was pretty impressive. She had worked her way up with the same company she'd had the internship with, all the way to a similar position as the one she would be taking on here. George had definitely had a good reason for hiring her.

"Why'd you leave?" I asked, looking up at her.

Rian sighed and shrugged. "You know how it goes," she said. "Corporate merger, company downsizing. I was the one to get cut."

I nodded. "Fair enough," I murmured, looking back at her résumé. That made plenty of sense, but it didn't explain what she was doing back here in Nebraska. There were other companies there in New York. She had made it very clear she had no desire to stay here any longer than she had to.

That in itself made me leery of agreeing to go through with the training process. What if we put in all the effort to bring her into the role here and she then up and quit?

I wouldn't know unless I asked her. I looked up at her. "If you don't mind me asking, what the hell are you doing back here?" The words came out a bit stronger than I had intended, but I hoped she realized that I wasn't playing around here. I wanted a serious answer from her. Her employment here was contingent upon it, in fact.

George may have hired her on, but if there was one thing that I wasn't going to do as a CEO, it was waste my time. If she didn't plan on sticking around, I wasn't going to put in the effort to train her.

Rian looked away for a moment, but when she looked back at me, there was enough of a challenge in her eyes that I could tell she wasn't lying to me. "Got tired of life in the big city, I guess," she said.

I wanted to believe her. To be honest, I knew how smart she was, and I didn't want to send her out of there before she had even really started. At the same time, though, there was something about the way she said it that sounded hollow to my ears. No, there was definitely more to it.

I had to decide whether I was willing to take a chance on her. If I was willing to trust her. I never wanted to trust her again.

At the end of the day, though, I had to accept the fact that George had hired her. Besides, we needed her, and as much as I didn't want to waste time training someone who was only there for the short term, I also knew that I didn't currently have the time to start interviewing other candidates for the position.

I started going over the company protocols with her, then took her on a tour of the office. As we walked around, I had to stop myself from watching the way her ass swayed in that sexy pencil skirt she was wearing. Jesus.

I couldn't possibly do anything about the attraction. And at the end of the day, I didn't want to. Still, I couldn't deny the fact that she looked damn good. It was definitely going to be hard to keep my mind on the job with her walking around the building.

What else could I do, though? I definitely couldn't fire her now, or she would claim that I had done so out of some sort of sexual harassment. I wasn't sure what the rules would be on that since I had slept with her long before I became her boss, but I knew that things would definitely be better if I found some flaw to the way she worked prior to firing her.

I had to quit thinking about her ass, her silky skin, everything else. I had to focus on work and keep things strictly professional. Suddenly, that felt like the most difficult thing I had ever faced with this company—and I had faced a lot on my road to becoming the company's CEO.

CHAPTER 2

RIAN

I knew I was staring, but I couldn't help myself. I had never expected to see Wes Brown again after college. I mean, there had been part of me that had definitely wondered what he was up to. I had thought about looking for him online a few times and maybe reconnecting. Just to see what he was doing with his life. I had decided against it each time, though.

It wasn't that I didn't care. But it definitely wasn't any of my business, and in any case, I had enough on my plate without inviting trouble into my life.

Now, though, I was kicking myself. If I had known he worked here, I would never have applied. I would never have even considered this company as a possibility. Finding out he was my new boss had me in full panic mode.

I had come to Nebraska looking for a fresh start. I had spent the last few years being ground down to nothing by my job, only to be tossed aside with no consideration when the company merged with a bigger one. I had come back to Nebraska because I still had some friends here from my college days, but I had thought that Wes would be long gone by now. It had never even occurred to me that he might work somewhere in town and that I might cross paths with him again.

After all, he had wanted that city internship just as badly as I did. It was part of why I hadn't told him I had gotten it in the end. I had been afraid to admit to him that not only was I leaving him behind, but I was also doing it so that I could take the position he had wanted most in the world.

If I had known he was going to be my boss, there were no ties in the world that would have brought me back here. Even if the rent on my new townhome was a fraction of what I had paid for what was practically a closet in the city. Even if I was lucky enough to not have to start at the bottom here and work my way back up again. Even if this new position paid me well enough to actually live.

As much as I'd wanted to go to New York City, I had grown kind of tired of the never-ending cycle of go, go, go. I was a different person now than I had been when I'd set off for the city.

For one thing, I was no longer living just for myself.

Coming back to Nebraska gave me the chance to spend a little more time with my daughter, and to raise her in an environment that I hoped would be a lot safer, quieter, and overall just better for her. I had spent a lot of time, when I first started looking into moving, researching different school districts and different opportunities for Ronny. I was sure this would be good for us, even though there was a part of me that still felt terrible for ripping my six-year-old away from all of her friends.

Of course, when I moved back here, I never imagined I would end up working for Ronny's dad. Ronny's dad who didn't even know that his daughter existed.

Seven years ago, it had seemed almost like a no-brainer to keep Wes out of things. He was halfway across the country from me, and anyway, we had never been in a relationship. It was just a one-night thing, the culmination of years of competition, leading to a blindingly passionate affair.

But that was all it had been: a one-night thing. I wasn't going to bog down his life with the knowledge that he had fathered a child. I knew that I could handle things on my own, and anyway, I wasn't sure that Wes and I could put aside our differences for long enough to raise a child together. Better I just handle things on my own.

Only that plan had hinged upon the idea that I would never see him again. Now that he was here in front of me, I couldn't help but wonder if I had made a huge mistake in never telling him.

As much as I hated to admit it, it wasn't wholly guilt that made me wish I had told him. It was also the fact that he was so damn attractive. Hell, he was hotter now than he had been when we were in college. How was *that* possible? Maybe it was something to do with the easy confidence he carried himself with, with the obvious power he wielded at the company. Or maybe it was more to do with the fact that his clothes were clearly tailored to fit him and his hair shorter than it had been, his messy kind-of-but-not-quite beach-boy look long gone.

Whatever it was, I immediately wanted him, and I couldn't help wondering what might have been if I had been up front with him about Ronny when I first found out I was pregnant. Would we have put together some sort of a relationship that transcended the realm of one-night stand? Where would we be now?

Except I knew only too well what would have happened. We had both been so young back then. We would have spent the first years at one another's throats about everything, sure that we both knew best when it came to how to raise our daughter. We would have driven one another crazy, and we would have ended up even further apart than we were now.

Or maybe not. With this secret between us, it was hard to believe we could be even further apart.

There was nothing I could do to change things now, anyway. I knew I couldn't get myself fired from this job after I had not only uprooted Ronny from New York but also put a down payment on a townhome. That meant I couldn't do anything to ruin things with my new boss. And that meant this secret had to stay a secret.

I tried not to feel too unsettled as Wes led me around the office. I knew that no one knew anything about me and that they had never met Ronny, but part of me kept expecting one of them to somehow out me to Wes as he introduced me. Of course, that didn't happen, but it was a relief to have Wes lead me into the privacy of my own office.

The view from here was a lot different from what I was used to, cornfields instead of high-rises, but I had to admit, it was comfortable and stylish. Better than I might have expected.

"I'll give you some time to settle in," Wes said, and from his tone of voice, it sounded like he was just as uncomfortable as I was with this whole situation but trying his best to remain professional. Good. I would do the same. "There's an all-staff meeting in a couple hours that I'd like you to attend, though."

"Sure thing," I said, heading over to the chair and flopping down in it, giving it a little spin. When I looked back up at Wes, he was staring at me. He seemed to give himself a little shake, then hastily backed toward the door.

I sighed heavily as the door closed behind him. I rubbed my fingers against my temples, already feeling a headache coming on. What could I do, though? Find another job? I probably should; even if Wes and I were trying to keep things strictly professional, I had a feeling that working for him was bound to end badly. But I knew there was nowhere else in town where I could find myself a similar position.

If I hadn't already put the payment down on the town-home, I might have seriously considered just going else-where. But as it was, and with Ronny in tow, leaving town wasn't an option. Doing something in another line of work had never been an option for me either. That meant that somehow, I had to make this work. For all our sakes.

I couldn't help thinking back to college, though. We'd gotten on one another's nerves all the time, it seemed like. We had gone up against one another for pretty much every opportunity that the business school had to offer, from internships to scholarships and more. Somehow, that had all culminated in that one night together, a night which I could never forget.

We had been at some house party celebrating the end of finals. It was the same day I'd found out I had gotten that internship in NYC. I'd had a few drinks and was dancing with a cute boy who had suggested that we go somewhere private to talk.

I still cringed thinking back to that night. I didn't know how I had gotten things so wrong. Had I really been naive enough to think that he really wanted to just talk? Of course that wasn't what he wanted…

I pushed at the guy's chest, trying to get him off me, but his mouth was still pressed against mine, his body pushing me back against the wall of the garage. We were totally alone here and in the dark. I could still hear the music from the party, the laughter, but it sounded strangely muted, as

if we were somehow underwater.

I distinctly heard the tear of my dress as the guy yanked it open to expose my black lace bra. It was almost as loud as the pounding of my heart and the alarm bells ringing inside my head.

That was as far as the guy got, though. Just then, the jerk was yanked away by a firm set of hands. Wes Brown was there, scowling at the other guy. "The fuck do you think you're doing?" he snapped.

For a second, I thought they were going to get into a fight. But as Wes stepped forward, looming over the other guy, it was obvious that it wasn't a fair match. The other guy took off. I slumped against the wall, fighting back the tears.

Wes Brown. Shit. I never thought I would be glad to see him of all people. It was undeniable, though—tonight, he had saved me.

I shivered with the cold, suddenly becoming aware of the fact that my dress was ripped. I hunched over, as though trying to hide the evidence. Wes was already shrugging out of his jacket. He held it out to me. I hesitated for a moment, looking up at his face, unsure what to do. He was carefully looking away from me, where most guys might have been drinking in the sight of my breasts while they had the chance.

I wordlessly accepted the jacket, the denim warm and soft in my hands. I buttoned it up all the way, covering all the evidence of what had happened. I folded my arms across my chest. Wes coughed lightly, uncomfortably, seeming like he didn't know what to say.

"Can I buy you a beer?" I asked, not wanting to talk about what had just happened and what he may or may not have seen. Wes raised an eyebrow at me, glancing back toward the noise of the party. "Not in there," I quickly said. "There's a place around the corner. Mulligan's."

Wes laughed. "Sure," he agreed. "Lead the way."

We walked quietly to the pub. It wasn't far, but it seemed like it took forever to get there. Neither of us seemed able to think of a way to break the ice.

As we sat there with our beers, though, we slowly started to open up to one another. I found out that he wasn't the monster I had thought he was. In fact, looked at in the right light, he was pretty charming. One beer turned into three, and the next thing we knew, it was last call.

"Let me walk you back home," he said as we spilled out onto the street.

I stared at him for a long moment, uncertain. I had managed, over the course of our time there, to forget about what had happened at the party, but now it all came rushing back. Was Wes trying to make a move on me?

Did I want Wes to make a move on me?

Before he could retract his offer, I nodded. "Sure," I said, turning my feet in the direction of home. Wes followed after me. Again, we were silent on the walk, but this silence was a lot more companionable than the one earlier in the night.

Back outside my door, I turned toward him, struggling to find the words to say to thank him for tonight. As I looked up at him, my breath caught. There beneath the light of the streetlamp, I had to admit he was handsome. It was something I had known for a while now, but I had buried my attraction behind our rivalry.

There was no rivalry to hide behind now. The next thing I knew, we were kissing.

I could feel the surprise radiating off him, but then he wrapped his arms around my waist and pulled me closer, deepening the kiss. Electricity shot through me, making me moan. My knees felt weak. Had I ever been kissed like this before?

No, I definitely hadn't.

He nipped playfully at my lower lip and then soothed the sting of pain with his tongue. My body tingled with pleasure, and it was all I could do to keep from ripping his clothes off right here.

I pulled back. "My roommate already moved out," I informed Wes.

He stared at me, and I could see the emotions warring in his eyes. I looked away bitterly. Oh, so he wasn't interested. Fine.

But Wes cupped my cheek in his palm, turning my gaze back toward him. "Are you sure?" he asked quietly, his eyes gentle as they met mine. Coming from anyone else, I might have scowled and pushed him away. I knew he was thinking back to earlier in the evening, though. To when he had come around the corner of the garage and saved me. He just wanted to make sure I was all right.

Something warm fluttered in my chest. I refused to look too closely at that, though. This was Wes Brown, and even though there was nothing left for us to compete over, it didn't mean we were suddenly friends. This was just sex.

And I wanted it.

I pulled him in for another kiss, this one vicious and searing as I tried to show him just how sure I was. As our tongues battled for dominance, I couldn't help but smile against his lips. Maybe there was one more thing for us to compete over.

And I wanted it. More than words could say.

CHAPTER 3

WES

Rian wasn't the first girl I'd kissed, but I had to admit, kissing had never felt like this before. From the very second our lips touched, it felt as though the air was sizzling around us. She approached kissing the same way she did everything else: with a fiery passion and a laser-sharp focus. It was one of the things that had earned my grudging respect in all those years having her as a competitor in business school. This was my first taste of what it felt like to have that focus turned on me, however.

It had me rock hard in no time at all.

I didn't want to pressure her, though. I didn't want to do anything that would make her uncomfortable. She wasn't trying to push me away like she had that jerk earlier in the night, but I definitely didn't want to be "that guy." We had had a few drinks, and Rian had never so much as looked at me in a sexual way before.

Then again, she was the one who initiated the kiss. She was the one who told me that she didn't have a roommate. She was giving me every signal that she wanted this. That, in itself, made the whole thing even hotter. How could I resist?

I let her drag me upstairs to her apartment. Our clothes went flying left and right, and we tumbled naked onto the bed. We *continued to kiss, but as our naked bodies moved against one another's, it gave the whole thing another dimension of lust. I groaned as she wrapped her hand around my throbbing length, and she grinned wickedly at me as she pulled back.*

Very deliberately, she guided my cock toward her entrance, a small fissure of concentration forming between her eyebrows. God, she was fucking adorable. How was I only now realizing it?

She wrapped her legs around my waist and pulled me closer to her until I was fully seated inside of her. Slowly, I started to rock my hips against hers, marveling at how tight she was and how perfectly I fit into her. How wet she was, too. It was as though her whole body was crying out for more.

I gave her everything I had, thrusting into her again and again, making her cry out, making her arch her back, making her shiver with desire.

In the present day, I woke with a gasp, my erection in hand, my body straining against the sheets. I was alone, though, with just the memory of Rian's body against mine. For a moment, I ached with the sense of loss, and it was like losing her all over again.

It was the third time this week I had woken up from that dream. Dream? Well, memory. It had all happened once. My mind seemed to recall every single detail.

I swallowed and rolled out of bed. As much as I tried to ignore my raging boner, though, I couldn't help but let my hand drift southward as I stood there in the shower. If I didn't take care of it now, I reasoned, there was no way I was going to make it through work. Not with her there in the same building.

After all, having her in the same building as me, knowing she was out there every single day, crossing paths with her every so often? That was the whole reason she was on my mind so much at the moment. Fortunately, our paths hadn't crossed much lately. No awkward elevator rides, and hardly any interaction in the hallways. I was counting it as a win so far.

These recurring sex dreams might be awkward, but at least they weren't totally out of control.

Which was why I nearly choked when I saw Rian's name on my schedule for that afternoon. I hurriedly clicked on the appointment and swore when I saw what it was. Of course. I was scheduled to take her out to lunch. It was a tradition that George had started, taking all the new managers out to lunch. In fact, this lunch had probably been set up back when George had first hired Rian when he was still the one in charge of the company.

I had no choice but to carry on the tradition. If I had seen this in my schedule sooner, I might have made some changes, decided that this wasn't the way I wanted to handle the company. If I canceled it now, though, people would wonder. Rian would wonder. I didn't want that.

The less that people talked about Rian and me, the better.

In any case, it was just lunch. What could possibly go wrong? We were hardly going to launch ourselves at one another and start ripping off the other person's clothes in public. We were both adults, and we could act like it. Still, the idea of being one-on-one with Rian was unsettling. Given our past history and my near-painful attraction to her, there were so many unfortunate ways that this could go.

There was a knock on my door, and when I looked up, Devin McKay was standing there. I forced myself to forget about Rian for now. It was too late to put off going to lunch with her. Might as well just face it as professionally as I could.

Speaking of being professional, Devin was one of the dozens of reasons why no one at the business could know that I had slept with one of our new managers, even if that had all happened a long time ago. The last thing I needed right now was a scandal. Not when Devin, a wealthy financier, was dangling millions of dollars in investment capital in front of me.

If things continued the way they were currently going, it was only a matter of time before the partnership I envisioned was finalized. I wouldn't do anything to risk that.

Not least of which because I liked Devin. We'd hit it off even from our very first meeting. The guy had a great sense of humor, especially about the sometimes dry business world. I was learning a lot from him as well. He had a ton of experience, and he really knew people in a way that was almost uncanny. I knew he had his own agenda and that that was why he was here, but I didn't think he was only looking out for himself. I had a feeling this partnership could be mutually beneficial.

A scandal could totally ruin things, though. So I pushed thoughts of Rian out of my head, or at least as much as I ever could these days.

Fortunately, the meeting with him went as well as they ever did, and at the end of it, I found myself shaking Devin's hand as he said he'd have his people draw up some preliminary plans for a partnership between our companies. To be honest, there was still a part of me that was in shock that it was all so easy. There was still a part of me that felt like I had to run things by George before I committed to agreements like that. But I was the CEO of the company at this point, and that meant I had the power to make those decisions.

George wouldn't have left me in charge if he didn't think I could handle it.

I was grinning to myself when Beth came to the door, a sour look on her face. "The new manager is in the lobby, ready to go to lunch with you," she said, and I glanced at my watch in surprise. I hadn't expected things with Devin to take so long. Was it really already time to take Rian to lunch?

I steeled my nerves. "Thank you, Beth," I said to my assistant. I'd been wondering if kindness could kill that mean streak inside of her.

Instead, her look darkened further. "No one ever takes assistants out to lunch," she said pointedly.

It startled a laugh out of me, and I immediately felt guilty as I saw her frown deepen. "If it's any consolation, I'm just doing this because it's a tradition that George set up with the new managers," I said, shrugging. Maybe that was a little too truthful, but the words were out of my mouth before I had a second to really think about them, and at that point, there was no taking them back.

"Anyway," I continued, "this isn't a social event. We're just going to discuss business."

Beth didn't look convinced, but I didn't have any more time to spend thinking about it. Rian was waiting for me. I suppressed the little thrill of excitement that went through me at the thought. *Business, not pleasure*, I reminded myself.

As I walked into the lobby, though, I was struck again by how beautiful she was. She was wearing a simple pantsuit, but somehow with her hair artfully tousled as it was, she looked like she had just stepped off a movie set. The high waist of the pants hugged her curves perfectly, and all I could think about was how I had missed her.

To tell the honest truth, I had tried to forget about her since college. It had hurt, the way she had just disappeared on me. I don't know what I had expected after that night, but I had at least thought she would say goodbye before she left.

I don't think I realized how much I liked her until that night. Until we were sitting across from one another in that bar, and the light caught her just right as she laughed over a beer. She had stirred something inside of me, and sleeping together that night had only cemented the feeling that she was something truly special.

Suddenly, I had to wonder if the whole reason I hadn't had a serious relationship since college had something to do with her. Not that I'd been holding out hope and waiting for her to come back, but maybe there was a little part of me that still hadn't gotten over her?

It was yet another unsettling thought, and one I knew I had to forget about. I was her boss, and nothing could ever happen. It would ruin everything I had worked so hard for since college, and I wasn't about to let it all go down the drain like that.

"How are things going?" I asked lamely as I walked up to her.

Rian shrugged, a cocky smile on her lips. "Well, you haven't heard anything bad yet, have you?" she asked teasingly.

I snorted and shook my head, leading her toward the door. "I'm not sure if that's comforting," I retorted. "The Rian I knew in college could lead a mutiny right under the professor's nose, and he would never know about it."

She laughed, but there was something guarded in her gaze. "Yeah, well, I'm not the same person anymore," she said, and there was a certain forcefulness to her tone.

It made me wonder what she must be thinking about me. Could she already tell I would be more than happy to have a repeat of that one night we'd had? Was I that transparent? I tried to act casual.

But as we sat down to lunch, I couldn't deny how awkward things were between us. Rian seemed to be trying too hard to focus on strictly professional topics. It wasn't just that she was acting like she had never met me before, but she was acting like neither one of us had a life outside of work. When I asked her what she thought of being back in Nebraska, she just gave me the clipped answer of "fine."

I pressed for more details, asking if she'd seen anyone

from college, if she still knew people from around there. Her noncommittal shrug gave me nothing to go on, so I quickly ended that line of conversation there.

Maybe it was for the best. If we didn't talk about our lives outside of work, we would have no choice but to keep things strictly professional. In fact, it was probably the best way to approach things.

Even if it did jar me a little. What had happened to the bubbly, vivacious girl I had known in college? I kept thinking about what she had said before about how she wasn't the same person as she had been back then. That was fair enough, but something big must have happened to her. She wouldn't have just turned into this person who was... honestly kind of boring.

Still, I allowed her to steer the conversation back toward work and the things she had been working on with her last company.

Didn't *that* make things awkward, though—talking about that? The reason she had gotten a position there was that she had somehow beat me out for that internship. I was over feeling upset about the fact she had snagged my dream out from under me. After all, if I had taken that internship, my life would be very different at this point. I probably wouldn't still be here in Nebraska, and at the end of the day, whatever I might have wanted when I was younger, I was happier here than I would have been in the big city.

So no, it wasn't that I was upset with her for bringing up the job because I still thought it should have gone to me. I was still upset that she hadn't said anything to me, though. That she had just disappeared.

"You know," I suddenly heard myself saying, "I would have at least expected you to say goodbye before you left town." Rian looked shocked, and then her face went through a complicated set of emotions. I refused to take back the words, though.

She should have said goodbye. That was the thing that had been eating at me all of these years. And that was the thing that made me so unsure about having her at the company now. Could I really trust that she wasn't the same person that she'd been back then? That she had changed, and that she was no longer likely to just disappear on me?

I wasn't sure. There was something she was hiding from me; I was more sure of that than ever before. There was a reason she was back here in Nebraska rather than back in New York with the life she had built for herself.

Until I knew what that reason was, I wasn't going to be able to trust her to stick around. As much as I hated to feel so negatively about this, that was the way things were.

CHAPTER 4

RIAN

I was doing all I could to enjoy the lunch. It was the first moment of alone time I'd had with Wes, basically, since that night back in college. I didn't think he had been avoiding me around the office, but our paths had barely crossed since I had started there. I couldn't help wanting to see more of him.

Okay, so there had been a part of me that was a little nervous when I saw this lunch appointment on my calendar. I knew we needed to keep things strictly professional between the two of us. The last thing that I needed was to lose my job over a dalliance that had happened years ago.

No, the last thing I needed was for him to find out he had a daughter. It was only going to confuse things if he found out about Ronny now. Although at the same time, I was starting to question my reasons for never telling him about her.

It all had to do with the very thing that Wes had asked me about now. Why hadn't I said goodbye to him when I was leaving?

It was a question I had struggled to answer ever since I

had left Nebraska, to be perfectly honest. Why had that one night meant so much to me? Was it just the fact he had rescued me? Or had something been building between us all that time without me even realizing it? Was it that easy for the respect I had for him as a businessman to translate into... something more?

I had been afraid that if I told him that I was leaving—if I tried to say goodbye—I wouldn't have had the strength to actually leave. It had taken everything I had to uproot myself from Nebraska and take off for New York City. I wasn't stupid; I knew I was going to have a hard time fitting in there. It was a whole different mentality, a whole different style of living. One I wasn't even remotely used to.

As exhilarating as it had been to find out I had been accepted into such a prestigious internship, I had been pretty well terrified. Something about that night with Wes had only made me realize just how much I was leaving behind.

What could I do, though? We had only had that one night together. It wasn't like I could turn down the internship—put my whole life on hold—just to see where things might go with him. Not least of which because I was sure he wouldn't have wanted me if I was the kind of person who would do that.

Besides, I knew he had wanted that internship. It would have felt too much like I was rubbing his face in it to tell him I was leaving for New York to essentially live out his dream. He was the whole reason I had even applied for that internship. He had been the one yammering about it one day in one of our classes, and when I'd pointed out that there was no way someone from Nebraska was getting accepted for it, he had challenged me to apply.

I hadn't realized how much I wanted it until I started the application process, but I wouldn't have started it if not for him. So no, I couldn't tell him about it before I left, even if I knew he was bound to connect the dots once I was gone. After all, I hadn't made any secret of it. It was right there in the school newspaper, in the list of all the graduating seniors and what they were up to after college.

Rian James: Internship at Tadwick Design Co. NYC.

I couldn't tell him, now, that the reason I hadn't told him I was leaving was that I knew he wanted that internship more than anything. It would sound too much like I was laughing at him for not getting it. And I definitely couldn't tell him that the reason I hadn't told him I was leaving was that I had been worried I was too attached to him after just one night together.

I didn't even know how he had felt about me back then. After all, I had been the one to initiate the kiss. I had been the one to all but drag him upstairs with me. Maybe he didn't care about me at all, and here I was, getting ready to give up an internship in New York just to see how things might go with him.

No, I couldn't do that. It would be ridiculous.

There was a deeper question, too. Why hadn't I called him once I was in New York? Well, that was just as messy. I had wanted to, but then I had found out about the pregnancy. How could I explain to someone on the other side of the country that I was pregnant? That it was an accident? That I hadn't planned for this?

It wasn't like he and I could just see if we were compatible as co-parents of a child, either. Either I would have had to move back to Nebraska, or he would have had to move to New York, all on the chance that things might not work out between us. While I definitely wasn't about to move back to Nebraska for him, I also felt selfish asking him to move to New York if he wanted any part of this child's life.

Besides, even before I met Ronny, I knew that there was no way I was sharing her with someone halfway across the country. I wasn't going to put her on a plane and go weeks without seeing her while she spent time with her father. Maybe that was selfish, but I felt sick at the very thought of doing that.

In any case, I wasn't in any sort of place in my life for a relationship right then. I was totally focused on the internship, loving every minute of it. I was determined to get a job with Tadwick once the internship period was up. I knew that in order for me to have any chance of getting that job, though, I was going to need to keep quiet about the fact that I was pregnant, at least at the time.

And if I was keeping it from the company, then there was no way I could tell Wes about it. I couldn't risk him showing up there out of the blue. I didn't know how I would explain that to everyone around me.

There was a deeper fear there, too. Wes and I had gone head-to-head on everything in college, and I knew he had wanted that internship. What if he wanted it so much that when I told him I was pregnant, he outed me to the company and destroyed any chance I had at getting a permanent job there?

When I thought back now, I felt kind of terrible for all the reasons I had left and all the reasons I hadn't told him about Ronny. They just seemed so selfish. At the same time, I knew I had been scared and that I hadn't been at my most rational. Still, how did I explain all of that to Wes now?

Thankfully, before I had a chance to, the waiter came, interrupting our conversation. I knew that wasn't the end of it all. I was going to have to keep my guard up around him if I didn't want him to find out about Ronny.

There was another thing: if I could go back and do it all over again, I might have made different decisions and decided to at least tell Wes about the pregnancy. Let him handle it however he wanted to. Having made the decisions I had, though, I knew that there was nothing to do but stick to them now.

If he found out about Ronny, he would never trust me again, and it could cost me this job. I couldn't have that. The stakes were too high. So our daughter needed to stay a secret.

After the waiter left, I turned the conversation back to the company and the rumors of investment capital. "Are you actually drafting an investment firm?" I asked bluntly.

Wes stared at me for a moment, and I could tell he was deciding how much he wanted to tell me. He definitely didn't trust me, even without knowing about the secret I had kept from him all these years. That was dangerous, with him as my boss and me as one of the managers at the company. We needed to find some way to work together, or else I was going to have to leave. There was no other option.

Which meant I had to find some way to earn his trust, or at least his grudging respect.

Wes finally nodded. "Yes, that's true," he said, beginning to tell me about Devin McKay and his plan to partner with us on a new product line.

As he spoke so nonchalantly about the project, I couldn't help but feel my blood begin to boil. I was new at the company, but for something like this, as the innovations manager, I should be spearheading the project. Especially since it sounded like it was the kind of idea that had only really taken off in the time I had been with the company.

If not spearheading it, though, I should have *at least* been brought on board and informed of what was happening. Devin McKay was known throughout the business world. He didn't take partnerships lightly, and this could be huge for the company.

From a personal standpoint, it was yet another blow to my ego. I got foisted out of my job in NYC, and now I wasn't part of the biggest innovation that my new company was going to be part of, possibly ever...

It's just because you're new, I tried to remind myself. I had to wonder, though, if things would have been handled the same way if George were still in charge rather than Wes. Or was he keeping me out of the McKay investment project out of spite? It was yet another uncharitable thought, but it made me realize that I didn't trust Wes any more than he trusted me.

I was the one with secrets, too. So maybe fair was fair.

Still, if I wanted to keep this job, I needed to speak up now. If I let him keep me out of this project, it was going to set up a precedent that I didn't particularly care for. As I opened my mouth to say something, though, my phone rang.

I glanced down at it, mouth already starting to spew the apology to Wes. My blood ran cold as I saw that it was Ronny's school calling me. *Shit.* As a mom, all sorts of horrific possibilities went through my brain in that instance. I had read all about what might happen if I uprooted her, all the things that could go wrong. She had seemed totally fine that morning. I had been keeping a close eye on her, watching for any changes in her personality that might suggest she was acting out.

If I hadn't seen anything of the kind, it either meant that I was a terrible mom and hadn't noticed the signs or that something else had happened to her. What if she was hurt? What if she was sick? I had come a long way since the panicked wreck I'd been the first time she was ever sick, but I still felt so helpless and sorry whenever she was sick.

I hated to say it, but if she was sick right now and it took me away from things at the job I had just started, it was only a matter of time before I accidentally said the wrong thing to Wes. That could cost me everything.

"Sorry, I have to take this," I said to Wes, already standing up and stepping away from the table. I would think of excuses later; for right now, I had to figure out what was going on with my baby girl.

Thankfully, nothing was as bad as I had imagined it might be. Ronny had taken a tumble out on the playground, but there were no broken bones to contend with or anything like that. However, she had been crying inconsolably for her mother, and I felt my heartstrings tug. She had been so easy going since we had moved there, but I couldn't help feeling like part of the reason she was so upset today was because she was in such a foreign environment, and that was all thanks to me uprooting her.

I had to be there. Which meant I had to come up with some kind of excuse.

I headed back into the restaurant and paused next to the table, summoning my nerves—and my best creative powers. "That was my property management company," I finally said, hoping the excuse was believable. "There was a water leak at our complex, and they're calling all of the tenants to come and assess the damage in our homes."

Wes looked worried as he got to his feet, tossing a handful of bills on the table to cover the lunch we had yet to receive. "That's terrible," he said, frowning. "Why don't you let me drive you home since I drove us over here."

I shook my head. The last thing I needed was for him to know where I lived. Besides, I wanted to go straight to Ronny's school to pick her up, not go all the way home and then out to her school. It would be quicker if he just brought me back to the office and let me take my own car. Not like I could tell him that, though.

"I don't know how long it's going to take," I said, continuing the lie. "And I'm sure you have things you need to do this afternoon?"

Wes winced. "Yeah," he admitted. "I have some meetings and things."

"Anything as interesting to product innovation as the Devin McKay one you had this morning?" I couldn't resist asking.

Wes stared at me for a moment and then winced. "Shit, Rian. I didn't mean to—"

"It's fine," I interrupted, because I didn't have time to have that conversation now. Somewhere out there, my baby was crying for her mother to come and get her.

Our baby.

It wasn't the time for that conversation either, though.

Wes nodded and led me back to his car so we could go back to the office. "Sure," he said, nodding. The car ride back was silent, and I wondered what he was thinking. Could he tell I was lying? This was one of the problems with not knowing him as well as I would have liked to: I just didn't know if he knew me well enough to know I was lying.

I couldn't think about that, though. Instead, the minute we were back at the building, I got in my car and then raced off to the school to pick up Ronny. She wasn't crying anymore by the time I got there, but her eyes were red and puffy and there were tear tracks on her cheeks.

I knelt in front of where she was sitting in the nurse's office, kissing her face repeatedly until she giggled. "Mama!" she shrieked, pushing me away.

I laughed. "There's my girl," I said affectionately.

Ronny's face wrinkled in consternation. "Do you have to go back to work?" she asked unhappily.

I thought back to the lie I had told Wes. I was torn between going back to work and taking care of my little girl. After all, I wanted to keep this job, but I had told him that it might take all day to resolve this. Besides, how often would something like this happen? I ought to just make sure that

Ronny was okay now and then put in some extra time some other day.

I shook my head, smiling at Ronny. "Nope," I told her. "I'm playing hooky this afternoon—and I'm taking you with me!"

Again, she giggled. "Yay!" she cried.

I scooped her up into my arms. "So, what are we going to do all afternoon?" I asked her.

Ronny's face screwed up in thought. "Could we go to the movies?" she asked.

I winced, trying not to let her see it. I wanted to say yes. If we were in New York, I would have said yes. But if we were in New York, no one would have seen us. Or at least, no one who knew me. It was tempting fate for us to go out in Nebraska that afternoon, after I had lied to my boss and told him I was going home to check on water damage in my place. Someone was bound to see us.

I hated lying to Ronny, but I heard myself saying, "I don't think there are any good cartoon movies out right now. Why don't we go home and watch some *Princess Patrol* instead?"

"Yeah!" Ronny cheered, wriggling in my arms with excitement.

I felt bad for lying to her. There were plenty of things we could have seen in the theater that day. But at the same time, it was a harmless lie. Besides, we were both comfortable curled up on the couch together, watching some of her favorite cartoons. Wasn't that what mattered?

I couldn't help wondering if maybe I should tell Wes about our daughter. Before he found out about her through some other sources. Ronny looked so much like me, but there were her eyes... Her father's eyes.

If I told him about her now, though, when he already didn't trust me, it spelled the end of my job. I couldn't do that to us now. I had to think about the bigger picture. Besides, keeping Ronny from Wes wasn't hurting her any. It was just... a different way of looking out for her.

I tried to push those thoughts out of my head as I settled in to watch movies with my daughter for the afternoon. I couldn't help feeling guilty, though.

CHAPTER 5

WES

I tried not to laugh as Devin tangled his fishing line for the umpteenth time. I tried to think if I had ever seen someone as inept at fishing as him. I didn't think I had. It made me wonder if he could even swim. Or what he would look like on ice skates. Nebraska and New York were totally different worlds.

It made me wonder how things had been for Rian in NYC and if that was part of the reason why she'd ended up coming back to Nebraska. I was trying not to think about her today, though.

"If you don't like fishing, we could have done something else," I told Devin, trying not to laugh.

He chuckled, though. "To be honest, I don't think I've been fishing since I was a kid," he said. "I remembered it being a lot more fun than this." He paused. "Of course, I also remember accidentally catching my brother's thumb as we were walking back to our campsite once, so maybe I don't remember things totally right."

I snorted. "Ouch."

"I think that was also the trip where my sister caught a snapping turtle and dropped the pole in the water and our uncle had to dive to recover it," Devin mused. "You know, when I think about it, I don't think I have a single fond memory of fishing from when I was a kid."

I laughed at that. "Not to be a shit, but you're pretty terrible," I said.

"For what it's worth, I appreciate that there's beer," Devin said, holding up a can in cheers to me.

I grinned and held up my can as well, clinking it against his. "I appreciate that we've come this far in our professional relationship that I can drag you out here," I said.

Devin laughed. "To be honest, I'm pretty happy to be here in Nebraska for a while," he said. "I can't say I knew much about it, but I like the lifestyle. Couldn't live here for very long, but I appreciate what you think is important to you."

"Like fishing?"

Devin shrugged, a devilish twinkle in his eye. "Maybe not. Not to mention, it's no wonder you're single," he said.

"Why's that?" I asked, grinning.

"You're up before dawn trying to catch fish, when there are perfectly good restaurants in town," Devin said, giving me a toothy grin.

I laughed. "Well, you're single, too," I reminded him. "What's your excuse?"

I intended it to be a joke, but instead, a strange look came into Devin's eyes, and I couldn't help but wonder if I had struck a nerve. I immediately felt terrible, but I didn't know how to ask if I had said something wrong. I knew I was already treading a thin line as far as this investment opportunity went. Devin McKay was known in the business world as someone who rarely attached his name to anything of any importance.

Had I just fucked thing up with him, just when things were really getting started? I didn't know how to ask.

Fortunately, Devin was the one to clarify things, before I could say anything. "As a workaholic, I don't have time for relationships," he said. I blinked, watching the lines rather than watching him. There was something in the way he had said it that made me wonder.

Was it that he no longer bothered with trying, or was it more that he knew that he didn't have the time and wouldn't bother trying? Was it more that he had never bothered losing someone, or that he had fallen in love, hadn't been able to work out his life with the needs there, and lost... or that he had never let himself fall in love in the first place?

I had to wonder. But of course, I couldn't truly ask. We just weren't on that level.

We headed back to shore after catching a few fish. It wasn't exactly the kind of day I had imagined, but when Devin suggested that we get brunch at a nearby place, I was hardly in the mood to argue with him. I wanted this partnership, and that was what today was all about.

That said, as soon as I started thinking about what brunch might lead to, I started wondering if maybe this wasn't the best idea. I remembered the look on Rian's face the other day during lunch, when I'd been telling her about the possible partnership. She wanted in on the partnership, and as our innovations manager, she deserved to be part of it, too.

I wasn't entirely sure how comfortable I was working that closely to her, but at the same time, I knew I couldn't exclude her. We were going to have to find a way to make things work on a professional level; there was no way around it. Why not start with that morning?

"If we're going for brunch, I should probably invite our

new innovations manager," I said to Devin. "It's about time you met Rian."

"Sounds good," Devin said easily.

I pulled out my phone to call Rian. I was surprised to hear her hesitate when I told her about the brunch, though. "I thought you were the one who wanted to be brought in on this project, or was I misreading things the other day?" I said, glancing over my shoulder to where Devin was patiently waiting a little ways away.

"No, it's good," Rian said. "I'll be there as soon as I can."

"See you soon," I said before hanging up.

Devin and I headed to the restaurant and got a table. "So tell me about this innovations manager," Devin said. "Rian, did you say it was?"

"Yeah, Rian James," I said, nodding. "George hired her on before he handed the company over to me. She did some work in New York City for a while, but she went to school here in Nebraska, so she knows the culture and all of that. Kind of a best of both worlds situation for you—she's not the kind of person who will take you fishing, I bet!"

Devin laughed. "I didn't mind the fishing," he protested. "Maybe it's not totally my cup of tea, but it wasn't terrible. But come on, I can tell there's something about Rian you're not telling me. Is she a horrible micromanager or something?"

I shook my head. "Nah, she and I just have some history, that's all." I said it as carefully as I could. I didn't want Devin to think I couldn't be professional about this. That might jeopardize the partnership. "We went to college together, at the same time. We went up for a lot of the same opportunities."

"Ah," Devin said, nodding. "And let me guess: once upon a time, you thought that you wanted to live in New York, too."

"Exactly," I said, relieved that he had deduced that much out without my having to admit I had been a little jealous of Rian way back then for getting the internship I'd wanted.

"Not much fishing to be done in the city," Devin said, grinning at me. "You would have been bored to tears. Or maybe you would have actually found yourself a wife."

I laughed. "Maybe. Or maybe I would have been one of those guys who went upstate every weekend to fish."

Devin shook his head. "Drive five hours for fish that you could have bought at the local shop? I don't get it."

Brunch continued in the same casual manner until Rian finally showed up. "Sorry I'm late," she said breathlessly as she sat down between the two of us at the table. "I wasn't expecting a brunch meeting on a Sunday."

"That's my fault," Devin said gallantly. "I'm sorry, I keep kind of unconventional hours. And today, I really wanted to try out this whole fishing thing that Wes has been telling me about."

"How'd that go?" Rian asked, grinning.

Devin shook his head. "It's a good thing I'm good at business or else my hypothetical future family would starve," he joked.

Rian laughed, and I felt a frisson of jealousy go through me at the sound. I tried to push it aside. This was just business; it wasn't like she would do anything as irresponsible as to sleep with him when we were on the brink of such an important partnership.

At the same time, my brain just couldn't shut up about the fact that they would make a cute couple. Devin was young and handsome, rich and powerful. He was everything a woman like Rian might be looking for in a guy. And as they swapped stories about life in New York, I couldn't help but feel left out.

I tried to ignore it, though. This was strictly professional.

Besides, why did I care? If things were going to progress between me and Rian, they would have a long time ago. It was too late for that now. Not least of which because she was my employee. No reason to be jealous. No reason to feel slighted.

CHAPTER 6

RIAN

"All right, I'm getting you out of the office for lunch," Angie, my assistant, announced, her hands on her hips as she stood in the doorway.

I looked up from my screen in surprise and then looked at the time, not even having realized that it was somehow already two in the afternoon. I gave Angie a sheepish smile. "I don't know what I'd do without you," I sighed. "Give me five minutes to get to a good stopping point?"

"Sure, but I'm timing you," Angie warned me.

In the time since I had started there, she and I had become fast friends, frequently going to lunch together. I had to admit, things were a lot crazier in the business than I had expected they would be. Who knew that sleepy little Nebraska had so much to do? Or maybe it was just the fact that I was still picking up the pieces from before I'd been hired. Apparently the innovations manager position had been open for a while, and things had definitely piled up.

Whatever it was, I was up to my eyeballs in work, and if it hadn't been for Angie and her amazing powers of organization, I would have really been struggling. As it was, I appreciated her little reminders, which were for everything from lunchtime to meetings to the most urgent things on my plate first thing in the morning.

She was a godsend, and I made sure she knew that.

"There's a new sandwich place on Newton Street," Angie informed me before I could ask where we were headed.

"Sounds great," I said, only just realizing how hungry I was. We ordered our food, and when it came, I practically inhaled mine.

We were just finishing up when Angie's phone rang. She glanced at the screen and grinned. "Mikey," she told me.

"Go ahead," I said, sure that her son wouldn't be calling her if it wasn't important.

She answered the call and chatted for just a minute before hanging up. "He wanted to go over to his friend's house after school," she explained. "They're working on some sort of science experiment or something? I'm just as happy for him to work on that at someone else's place!"

I laughed. "I can imagine," I said. "Ronny had a water-cycle project last year, and I thought I was being clever, but long story short, our house smelled like burned plastic for a week! I totally understand now why all the projects at that age tend to look exactly the same."

Angie looked surprised. "I didn't realize you had a kid," she said.

Shit. A part of me wanted to lie and tell her that Ronny was my niece or something. Then again, it wasn't that big of a town. People were bound to find out that Ronny existed sooner or later, and I didn't want to lie to Angie now and have it bite me in the ass later. Besides, I was so sick of having to keep this secret from everyone. I needed to confide in someone.

I made the split-second decision to tell her about Ronny. "I have a daughter," I said, trying to pretend that telling her wasn't giving me a mini freak-out. "You can't tell anyone at work, though. Please. I need you to promise you'll keep it a secret."

Angie raised an eyebrow at me. "If you're worried that they won't keep you around if you have to take time off because she's sick or something like that, you don't need to worry," she said. "I don't know how things were done in New York, but they're different here. They'll work with you however they can." She paused. "I mean, aren't they legally required to do that?"

"It's not that," I sighed. I should have known that she would ask. I bit my lower lip. Again, though, I just wanted someone to know everything. I wanted someone who I could talk to about this. "Wes is her father. He doesn't know that, though."

Angie's eyes widened. "Oh wow," she said. "Wait, how old is your daughter?"

"She's seven," I said. "Wes and I knew one another in college. We only slept together once."

"Is that why you came to work for the company?" Angie asked.

I shook my head quickly. "No, of course not," I said. "I didn't know that Wes worked here. He and I haven't talked since college. I just happened to be looking at coming back to Nebraska, and when George hired me, it seemed like the perfect fit."

Angie whistled quietly. "Yikes," she said. "That must be tough for you. Do you think you're going to tell Wes about her?"

"Not yet, for sure," I told her. "Later? I don't know. Maybe. I need to see how things go first, though. Like I said, I didn't know that he worked here or else I wouldn't have done this to myself. I already uprooted Ronny once, though, and I can't do that again so soon. She still doesn't really have any friends here, and I would feel terrible making her start over *again*. I need to keep the job."

"That makes sense," Angie said, nodding. "Well, your secret is safe with me." She paused. "But you know, my youngest is also seven. I bet Brian and Ronny could be friends."

I grinned. "That would be awesome," I told her. "Why don't we arrange a playdate?" I had some misgivings about Ronny getting too close to my work life, but at the same time, it would be great for Ronny to have a friend here. Besides, Angie knew the whole truth and had promised to keep my secret. She wasn't the one I had to worry about. It wasn't like the kids would be playing there in the middle of the office or anything.

I headed back to work with a lighter heart, just in time for that afternoon's meeting with Wes. When I got to his office, though, his assistant Beth told me he was on a phone call and asked me to wait.

"Sure thing," I said, dropping into a seat.

Beth pursed her lips as she stared at me. "I bet you're missing New York City, huh?" she asked, apropos of nothing.

I looked at her in surprise, wondering if Wes had said something to her. But I hadn't so much as hinted to Wes that I didn't want to be there in Nebraska. In fact, I was really enjoying being back here. The pace of life was refreshing, and I was realizing that it was a much better place for me to raise Ronny.

"I mean, Nebraska is so dull, isn't it?" Beth pressed. "Hardly any nightlife. Pretty much no shopping either."

I shrugged. "I went to college here," I told her. "I knew what I was getting myself into before I came back here."

"Sure," Beth said. "But I guess you probably wish you had a better job, right? Something higher profile, with better pay? I'm sure you weren't making this little in the city."

I stared at her for a moment, wondering if there was some sort of motive behind her questions or if she was just curious. The inquiries were borderline rude, though. Before I could call her out on it, Wes opened his office door and called me in. Was it my imagination, or did Beth's face darken as I walked past?

I shook those thoughts out of my mind. Wes and I had a lot to work on, and I didn't have time for any sort of office drama. Which was another reason I was trying so hard to keep everyone from finding out about Ronny, I told myself. It would only complicate things.

Right now, Wes and I were working hard on the new product line that we were pitching to Devin. We dove right into it that afternoon and kept working on it long after everyone else went home. It was hard to quit when we were being so productive. That said, around six, when it became clear that we weren't finishing anytime soon, I snuck out "to go to the bathroom" and called the daycare service that watched Ronny in the afternoons after school.

Fortunately, they told me that they had no problem keeping her a little while later. I went back into the office and dove into the work again.

A little while later, Wes was sketching out an idea, and I leaned over to take a closer look. His hands were just as talented and just as sure as they had been back in college. I found myself suddenly mesmerized by the look of his fingers as he brought his ideas to life on the paper.

I could feel the heat of his body across the space between us, and suddenly all I could smell was his cologne, a familiar scent from college. I found myself thinking back to that night that we'd had, and when Wes turned to face me, it was only natural that my eyes were drawn to his lips.

Wes noticed it, too, and then the next thing I knew, he had grabbed me, dragging me into his lap and kissing me passionately. I moaned against his lips, unable to get over how perfectly we fit against one another.

I felt drunk on passion already. How had I gone seven years without him, in the time since that first night together? Now, I let myself fall into the feeling of it, reveling in the way his fingers teased their way up underneath my shirt. It was all I had needed for so long, and I wasn't thinking about all the reasons we shouldn't be doing this.

I gave myself over to him. And as he fiddled with the buttons on my shirt, I knew there was no going back.

CHAPTER 7

WES

Having Rian alone in my office had been damnably distracting, all afternoon long. It had taken everything I had to focus on my work and not on the way she grinned when she thought she had a particularly great idea, or the way that the tops of her breasts looked as she bent over to look closer at what I was doing, or the way that her hair brushed her cheek as she frowned in concentration.

She was adorable and sexy and undeniably attractive all at the same time. I was trying to go over all the reasons why I couldn't just grab her and bend her over my desk, but seeing the way she stared at my lips was just too much for a man to take.

I pulled her into my lap and kissed her. She opened her mouth to me immediately, body begging for me to have her. She kept moving against me, abortive little shifts of her hips, and I could tell she was waiting impatiently for me to take her. How could I resist that? I wasn't made of stone, and as much as I'd been trying to focus on work all day, there was something about watching her move, watching her explain her ideas, watching her watch me with that look of intense concentration on her face—well, I had spent the afternoon half-hard, and my erection was impossible to ignore now.

I lifted her out of my lap and set her down on the edge of my desk. She spread her legs, her pink panties on full display as her tongue absently traced her lower lip, which was flushed and swollen from our impromptu make-out session. I continued to watch her face as I pushed her panties aside and plunged my fingers inside of her.

As I'd expected, she was wet as could be, body desperate for my intrusion. Her mouth opened into a little O of surprise, and she arched her back, pushing down onto my digits in wanton desperation.

I growled and stepped into the space between her legs, melding my mouth with hers once more as I continued to work my fingers inside of her, plying her folds, opening her up to me. She clung to me, her fingers gripping tightly at my shoulders as though she was holding on for dear life.

I fumbled at my belt with my left hand and undid it and my slacks, letting them fall to the floor—but not before I fished a condom out of my wallet. I had to pull my fingers out of her so that I could open the shiny foil wrapper. Rian whined, her pussy clenching around nothing, and I couldn't help grinning at her desperation. She didn't seem at all self-conscious, though.

And god, wasn't that sexy. She was making no attempt to hide how much she wanted it, and that only stoked my own desperation ever higher.

I rolled on the condom and thrust into her without a second moment of hesitation. Her hands spasmed against the desk, wrinkling papers there. I didn't care now. Whatever we ruined, we could redo again, and better. Right now, the only thing I cared about was this beautiful vixen pressing her body up against mine.

"Oh fuck," Rian said reverently, her whole body shuddering with pleasure as I began to move inside of her. "*Yes.*"

I grinned, unable to help it. Not that I was in any better shape than she was. I already felt as though I might blow my load, and we had barely gotten started. I instinctively slowed down, wanting to drag this out, wanting this to last.

After all, this might be the only chance I got to show me everything that she meant to me. With the way she had disappeared last time we slept together, who knew what this would bring.

Rian opened her eyes and fixed them on mine, an intense and unreadable look there in her darkened gaze. She wrapped her fingers around my bicep, pulling me closer, her other palm flat against the desk for leverage as she moved with me. She gasped out my name, shuddering as her pleasure spiked ever higher.

We came at the same time, bodies both singing with feeling. My body trembled with the strength of release, and Rian fell back against the desk, panting softly for breath.

In the aftermath, I felt as though I was coming back into myself, staring down at her as though she was someone I hardly knew. A stranger. Which, to be honest, wasn't too far from the truth. Suddenly, all of my earlier misgivings came rushing back. Who knew if she planned on staying at the company. Who knew what she was thinking. She could disappear again tomorrow, and I would have nothing left except memories. *Again.*

It was going to be even more difficult to forget what had just happened. This edge of desperation made things even more intense than the previous time we'd slept together. Or maybe it was the sheer naughtiness of it all. She was my *employee*. This wasn't supposed to happen.

But it had.

For a split second, I was tempted to invite her home with

me that night. I wanted to taste her. I wanted to take her over and over again, until she was raw and spent and unable to cum anymore. I wanted to give her everything and then some, to drive her to the brink again and again.

Just as the words formed on my lips, however, I heard the sound of a vacuum cleaner outside of my office. We both jerked to attention, hurriedly beginning to pull on our clothes, like teenagers who had been caught in the middle of the act. Neither of us could look the other in the eye, and neither of us spoke.

Fuck. What the hell had just happened? I knew better than this. I should never have given in to the temptation. It was entirely inappropriate.

I forced myself to turn to face Rian. There was a part of me that wanted to pull her close, to hold her, to brush back that stray lock of hair, to feel the softness of her cheek beneath my palm again. I couldn't do that, though. I just couldn't.

I shook my head slowly. "We can't," I said quietly, trying not to read too much into the complicated set of emotions that rushed across her face at the words. I forced myself to grit out the rest of it: "We have to keep things strictly professional between us. What just happened was a mistake." I could see the protest in her eyes, and I shook my head again. "I'm your superior," I reminded her. "A relationship between us would be entirely inappropriate."

Rian stared impassively at me for a long moment, but finally she nodded. "I understand," she said. "No relationship beyond a work relationship." She matter-of-factly started collecting her things. I wanted to stop her, to tell her that she didn't have to rush out of there. We could go back to what we had been doing before, keep working on things.

In any case, though, it was late. Besides, I had a feeling if I kept her in there for any longer, it was only a matter of time before one of us slipped again. We couldn't do that.

Still, I had to admit that watching her hurry out of there without a goodbye or a backward glance hurt. It was silly to feel as though I was the one who had been rejected. After all, I had been the one to remind her that we couldn't do this.

It felt a little too much like being left behind in Nebraska back after college, though. It felt a little too much like that other time she had left without saying goodbye. What else could we do, though? There was no way we could get away with a relationship; it would be risking both of our jobs, everything we had ever worked for. At the end of the day, I knew that we were both too driven and career-minded to ever risk something like that.

CHAPTER 8

RIAN

I was surprisingly nervous before going into the pitch meeting with Wes and Devin. I supposed it made a certain amount of sense. I used to feel confident as anything when it came to work things, but getting fired had been a real kick in the teeth and my confidence wasn't what it used to be.

I was trying to pretend that was the only thing that had me feeling unsettled. I knew that was a lie, though. What I was really afraid of was that everyone would be able to tell what had happened between Wes and me. I knew that was ridiculous. We were old enough to be able to act like adults about the situation. Still, I couldn't help second-guessing every look that he and I shared. Were we acting too formal? Too friendly? I realized that I didn't know what normal felt like with him. During college, our rivalry had taken precedence over everything else, and since coming here, well.

I couldn't allow myself to imagine what "normal" with Wes might feel like. I was afraid that that normal might feel a little too much like love.

I wasn't thinking of that now, though. If there was one

thing I was good at, it was focusing on the pitch to the exclusion of all else. I had worked too damn hard on this to let myself get distracted now.

I gave it all I had, pitching our ideas for the product line and how much investment we were going to need to roll it out. I was so hopeful that we would be able to secure the funding. Sure enough, Devin was nodding at the end. "I really like the idea," he said. "Unfortunately, it's not wholly up to me, and I do need to advocate to the board for it."

Even though I knew it wasn't 100 percent yet, I had to admit, I felt excited, like I had pulled in a major win for the company. And when Wes smiled at me, I nearly melted. It felt good to have my hard work recognized, and it was something I was realizing my previous company had rarely done.

"I want both of you with me when I present the idea to the board, though," Devin added. "They respond better when they know exactly who they're doing business with, and I like the passion that you brought to the pitch. I think they'll respond to that." He paused. "I've got a private jet, so we could go out to NYC when I'm scheduled to on Sunday. I know I'd be pulling away two of the top people in the company, though, so rest assured that we'll get you back as soon as we can."

He said it with a smile on his face, like he was sure we would both jump at the opportunity. And I had to admit, there was a part of me that was excited at the idea of going back to New York, even for a short time. I had been away for long enough now to realize all the things I missed. Like the amazing vegan Chinese food place that had been around the corner from my old apartment.

It wasn't only me I had to think about, though. I couldn't just up and leave my daughter, go jetting off to NYC on a business trip with her alone at home. She was too young for that still. Except at the same time, I couldn't bring Ronny with me, not with Wes and Devin being there. It would have been one thing to sneak her out there with me if we were flying commercial. On a private jet, there would be no hiding.

So I found myself protesting, trying to convince Devin that it didn't make any sense to fly us both out to New York for this. "It would be way more cost-effective for us to help with the presentation through video-chat," I pointed out. "I'm sure the board would still get a good idea of what we're about."

Devin shook his head, though. "These guys, a lot of them are a little, shall we say, old-fashioned," he said, shrugging unapologetically. "I know that they'd get a good idea of what you're like that way, but they'd feel more comfortable if you were there in person. Unless there's some reason you can't come?"

For a second, one panicky instant, I wondered if he somehow knew what I was hiding. But his expression was merely curious, not accusatory, and I realized he was joking. I had to stop taking things so seriously. Still, it was hard to feel calm right now. What could I say?

I turned to Wes, deciding that appealing to him was my better bet. Surely his business sense would be against this. Besides, there was no way that he wanted to be alone with me in New York, in light of what had happened in his office while we were working on this pitch. He had to realize that it would be dangerous.

For a moment, I let myself think back to that night. God, it had been good. Even better than before. It was clear he was more experienced than he had been back in college, but it was more than that. There was something about knowing that he was the father of my daughter, that we had this undeniable connection that transcended that moment. It made it all the more special to be sleeping with him.

Even if it was just carnal lust drawing us together right then. Even if he didn't even know about Ronny's existence.

I had to admit, it had hurt that he was so quick to tell me that it could never happen again. I knew, logically, that he was right. But something about the way he had said it—about the fact that he had called it a *mistake*—that just bothered me.

I couldn't think about that now, but I hoped he thought that that was my reason for not wanting to be in New York alone with him. I hoped he agreed that we were better off if only one of us went, and if that one person was him.

"You don't really want both of us to go, though, do you?" I asked him. "I mean, I don't know a ton about the company structure yet, but it does seem like overkill for both of us to go to New York. I'm just starting to get into the swing of things here, to be honest. I don't want to lose the momentum that I'm feeling here."

Wes frowned at me and then glanced apologetically at Devin. For a second, I thought I had won him over that easily, but then he turned that apologetic look back on me and said, "I do think it would be better for both of us to go to New York," he said. "Or if only one of us is to go, it should be you. You're the one who delivered the pitch with so much enthusiasm, and I think Devin's right: if anything's going to win over the board, it's the fact that you clearly care about this product line."

He paused and then shrugged, grinning crookedly at me. "Besides, I would have thought you'd jump at the chance of going back to New York. As for me, I'd much rather stay here. I'm not much of a city person."

I stared at him for a moment, trying to come up with some way to explain why I couldn't go. What excuse could I give, though, short of telling them about Ronny? I was backed into a corner.

Slowly, I nodded. "Okay," I said. "Then we'll both go." I'd just have to figure something out. I couldn't lose this job, and I couldn't admit to them that I had a seven-year-old daughter I had been hiding from them. Not least of which because it would be only too easy for Wes to do the math, when he found out how old Ronny was, and figure out that the girl was his.

I walked back to my desk in a daze. "Whoa, what happened in there?" Angie immediately asked, coming into my office and shutting the door behind her.

I slumped into my chair, pressing my fingers against my closed eyelids. "Devin loved the pitch," I told her.

"Isn't that a good thing?" Angie asked skeptically.

"Sure," I said. "Only he loved it so much that he wants me and Wes to go with him to New York to make the pitch to the board."

"So?" Angie asked, not connecting the dots. "Is there some reason you don't want to go back to New York? Or do you know someone on the board from your previous job or something?"

I shook my head. "No, but I can't just jet off to New York and leave Ronny here," I pointed out. "It's not like I can take her with me, though."

Angie's confusion evaporated, and she smiled at me. "Oh, that," she said, as though it was nothing. "Don't worry about it. I'd be happy to watch Ronny for you while you're gone."

I stared at her for a moment, surprised. Then, relief rushed through me. "That would be awesome," I said gratefully. I wasn't thrilled with the idea of it still, but at least I knew that I could trust Angie. She had three kids of her own, after all—three boys, even. She knew what she was doing when it came to taking care of kids. Still...

"I've never been away from Ronny for that long before," I admitted nervously.

"I know that feeling," Angie said. "When Nico was three, my mom got sick and I had to leave him with his dad for two weeks while I went to take care of her. It was one of the hardest things I've ever done. Every time they called me and Nico asked when I was coming home, I felt like my heart was breaking." She paused. "But we'll video-chat you every night, don't worry about it. It'll still be hard, but she'll be all right. You both will be."

I smiled at her, grateful for her support. "Thanks," I said.

Angie waved my thanks away. "You just focus on the presentation," she said. "After all, you're going to be representing the whole company. If you land this investment, it could mean big things for all of us."

I grinned. "Yeah, it could," I agreed, feeling a little glimmer of that earlier excitement come back to me.

Still, telling Ronny about it was difficult. I crouched down next to her as she sat on the couch that evening. "Sweetie, Mommy needs to go away for a work thing for a few days," I told her.

Ronny cocked her head to the side. "How far away?" she asked. "Like on a big airplane like when we were coming here?"

"Just like that," I said, deciding not to tell her that I was headed back to New York. She would probably want to know why she couldn't come with me to see all of her friends there, and I wouldn't know how to explain it to her. She didn't know anything more about her father than Wes knew about her, and I planned to keep it that way, at least for now.

"Do I have to stay at school forever and ever?" Ronny asked.

I suppressed a smile. "Nope," I promised her. "Angie said you could stay with her and the boys."

Ronny's eyes brightened. "Like a long, long, long, long sleepover?" she asked.

"Just like that," I said, nodding, amused to see she wasn't upset at all.

"Okay," Ronny said, sitting back, smiling happily. "They're fun. And they've got a dog!"

I smiled as well, unable to help how tinged with sadness the expression was. I was relieved she wasn't upset, but at the same time, it was hard to accept the fact that my baby was growing up and didn't need me as much anymore.

I supposed it was only a matter of time before she started to take after me. I had always been an independent kid, and I had seen flashes of that in Ronny already. She had never cried as much as other babies seemed to. She had always wanted to learn how to do things on her own, from tying her own shoes to making her own toast.

Still, it was a bittersweet moment and got me thinking about how much I would miss if things continued along this track. If I kept leaving her for business trips, how much more independent would she get? Was I ready for that?

There was no going back now, though. This was the reality of our situation, and the only thing I could do was accept it. Still, I climbed up to sit next to her on the couch, wrapping an arm around her and snuggling close as I watched the cartoon on the screen with her. For at least a little while longer, she was still my baby girl. I would take those moments for as long as I could get them.

CHAPTER 9

WES

I settled into my seat on Devin's private jet, luxuriating in how comfortable the oversized seat was. This was way better than flying commercial, I had to admit. It was my first time on a private jet, and I found myself wondering what it would be like to be rich enough to have one of my own.

One of the things I liked about Devin, though, was the fact that even though he had a ton of money, he never seemed pretentious. He had even been willing to go out fishing with me while he was there in Nebraska, and even though he hadn't been much good at it and even though he had admitted that he didn't particularly understand the point of it, at the same time, he was good-natured about it.

Maybe there wasn't as much of a difference as I had always thought between people who were filthy rich and, you know, the rest of us. Or at least, maybe money wasn't the only thing that made a difference there.

I glanced over, watching Rian and Devin chatting. Devin was asking Rian about the places she was planning to go once she was back in the city. They were laughing and joking, and it all seemed so... effortless. They had way more in common with one another than Rian and I had ever had. I felt jealousy well up inside of me again.

I knew it was foolish. I couldn't have Rian. That just wasn't to be. At the same time, though, I didn't want to see anyone else with her, even if that man was my friend. I didn't want to watch her flirting with someone else. Especially not if that man was handsome and rich and probably the best kind of guy for her.

It wasn't like I could say anything about it, though. I suddenly wished that I had agreed when Rian tried to tell me that we didn't need to both come to New York. It would have been so easy to agree with her and tell her to stay in Nebraska while Devin and I went to the city alone. But I knew the pitch would go ten times better with her at the forefront of it, and besides, she deserved to be the one making the pitch. She had put a lot of work into it, paying close attention to the details and fine-tuning everything.

She deserved to be the one to get a taste of success if—no, when—the board agreed to invest. I couldn't deny her that, and especially not because I didn't want her to spend more time around Devin than she already had.

Besides, I was counting on her being there with me in New York. I had always felt out of my depth there. I didn't know where to go for dinner, I didn't know what to do in between the meetings, and I just couldn't shake the feeling that I was out of place. I was counting on her to help me feel more like I belonged there, as silly as that sounded.

Now, though, I wondered whether she wouldn't just spend all her free time with Devin. Another surge of jealousy rose up inside of me, but I pushed it aside. I had no right to feel possessive of her. I was her boss, nothing more. I couldn't be anything more.

We finally landed at the airport, and Devin had a limo waiting there for us. He dropped us at a swanky hotel downtown, where his people had already made reservations for us. I had to admit I was impressed.

Rian looked impressed, too. "God, the check-in counter is bigger than the apartment I had when I lived here," she joked.

I laughed. "Yeah, this is pretty crazy," I said. We went up to our rooms, which happened to be right across the hall from one another.

"I guess we should freshen up," Rian said, lingering in the hallway and staring questioningly at me. "What time did Devin say he was picking us up for dinner again?"

"Six," I told her.

"Cool," Rian said, still lingering, looking like she didn't know what to say. I felt the same way. I couldn't seem to stop thinking about all the things that could happen while we were on this business trip, if we both just gave in to the temptation. I knew we couldn't do that, but holding myself back was so difficult at the same time.

"I guess I'll see you in a little while," I forced myself to say.

"Yeah," Rian said, and I wondered if she was thinking the same thing as me. She certainly scurried quickly into her room at that point.

I headed into my own room, shutting the door deliberately behind me. I knew I couldn't let myself do anything to her on this trip. It was enough that we'd fucked in my office. We couldn't go there again. Still, as I got in the shower, the water cascading around me, I found myself thinking about her again, imagining her there in the shower with me, water tracing patterns across her silken skin.

I brought myself off in my hand, feeling dirty and dissatisfied. My hand did little to ease my desire for her. But I knew that making love to her wouldn't be right. It couldn't happen again.

I got out of the shower and toweled myself off, trying to put those thoughts out of my mind.

I couldn't help feeling breathless a couple of hours later when I met Rian and Devin down in the lobby, however. Rian was wearing a slinky red dress with a low back, and she looked incredible. I didn't think I had ever seen her dressed so sexily before, and it was all I could do not to launch myself at her.

As we headed to the restaurant and were seated at a quiet table at the back, I had to keep reminding myself not to stare at her. There was something about her tonight, though, and it wasn't just the way she was dressed or the artful makeup making her eyes look brighter than usual. She belonged here, and there was something about watching her that just made me ache for her.

She was like a candle and I felt like a moth, drawn to her brilliant energy.

At dinner, Devin sprang for an expensive bottle of wine, and as I drank, trying to forget about my desire, I found that instead my thoughts turned distinctively naughty. We spent the early part of the evening talking business, but soon things became more casual. Rian started talking about our old business school rivalries, and Devin laughed his head off.

I found myself laughing just as much, even though looking back now, I couldn't believe I had wasted all that time with her. What if things had been different? What if I hadn't been blinded by the hopes that I had for my career and I had instead focused on Rian and how beautiful and smart and witty she was?

Things could have been so different. I felt a pang of sadness go through me at the thought.

There was no changing it now. There was no changing the fact that I hadn't noticed what I had until it was gone. There was no changing the fact that I hadn't called her when she'd disappeared like that, no changing the fact that I had just let her go like she didn't matter to me at all.

There was no changing the fact that I was her boss now and that nothing could ever happen between us. No changing the fact that I could look but would never be allowed to touch again.

As I watched her and Devin laughing with one another, I faced the reality of the situation: that I was doomed to lose her again. I was going to have to watch as she went off with someone else. My thoughts turned melancholy, and even though I knew we were here to celebrate the fact that at least the initial pitch had gone well, that Devin liked our ideas and wanted to move forward with them, this weekend wasn't going to end totally joyfully.

It just couldn't. And there was nothing I could do about that.

CHAPTER 10

RIAN

I had to admit, I liked the way the night was going. I knew the dress I was wearing was a bit risqué. It was worth it to see the way Wes's eyes kept straying toward me. I could tell he was trying not to stare, but he wasn't being totally successful at it. He wanted me. That was a heady feeling.

I knew nothing could happen between us. That I was playing with fire. At the same time, though, it felt good to know he wanted me, in spite of the way he had been so quick to tell me the other day that nothing could ever happen between us again.

I had to admit, it was equally affirming to get Devin laughing like that. So sue me—he was handsome and rich, and it was doing wonders for my confidence to have both of the guys laughing and grinning. We might be here for business, but I hoped to have a little fun as well. I was starting to realize just how little adult time I'd had since Ronny was born. While I loved cuddling on the couch with my daughter and watching cartoons, maybe I needed to look into having a babysitter every so often and maybe going out for drinks with Angie or things like that.

Devin's laughter was interrupted as his phone started ringing. He answered it in a clipped tone, his face stormy before he'd even heard a word from the person on the other end. "I'll be right there," he barked into the phone after a moment. Wes and I exchanged glances, both of us wondering what was up.

Devin stood up. "Sorry, I have to go," he sighed. "It's a bit of an emergency."

"Is everything all right?" I asked tentatively.

"I'll be fine," Devin said immediately, his tone grim. "But someone else won't be. Enjoy the rest of dinner, and I'll talk to both of you tomorrow." He turned and left before either Wes or I could say anything else.

Wes and I exchanged another glance. What the hell had that meant? Devin would be all right, but someone else wouldn't be? It was a side of the man I hadn't seen so far, not that I knew him well. It made me wonder what kind of a businessman he really was. Was he truly the kind of man we wanted to tie our company with?

Suddenly, though, I realized the folly of my thoughts. "Our" company? It wasn't my company at all. This decision was wholly up to Wes and what direction he wanted to take with the business. And clearly, he wanted to work with Devin. I was just along for the ride.

I had to wonder, though.

"Well," Wes said brightly, "there's no reason to let the rest of this wine go to waste." He leaned in conspiratorially. "It's an expensive vintage, you know."

I laughed. "Yeah, when he ordered it, my eyes nearly bugged out of my skull," I admitted.

"Mine too," Wes said, chuckling. "I hoped no one noticed, because I definitely felt like a country bumpkin." He leaned back, sipping at his glass. "I hope I'm not spoiling you when you're so new to the company, but things aren't usually like this. I mean, we do a fair business, but this is definitely one of the bigger investors that we've ever acquired."

I grinned. "Yeah, this is pretty intense," I said.

"But I guess you're used to this kind of thing with the company you worked for in New York?" Wes added.

I shook my head, frowning. "To be honest, they never really... Well, there just wasn't the same kind of recognition of the workers, I guess," I said slowly. I didn't want to throw the company under the bus, but at the same time, I wanted Wes to understand how much I appreciated his approach to the company. "If there was any wining and dining to be done," I finally said, "it was the executives at the company who did it, even if they weren't really involved with the project. I just gave a lot of presentations and things."

"Huh," Wes said, looking thoughtful. "That kind of sucks."

I laughed. "Yeah, kind of," I agreed. I was quiet for a moment. "I like that you're involved in everything. You don't micromanage either, though. It's just, I don't know. I like it."

Wes flushed slightly—was that from the wine or from the compliment? He changed the topic of conversation back to college, and I let him. We polished off the rest of the second bottle of wine and then headed back to the hotel, which was only a short walk away.

It was good to be with Wes, I had to admit. I knew he was off-limits, but there was something about being with him that made me feel safe and somehow cared for. It was partly the attention he had lavished on me both of the times we'd had sex. It had seemed like he was watching out for me, like my pleasure was at least as important as his own.

But it was also things like this: as we walked back to the hotel and I suppressed a shiver, he slipped out of his jacket and wrapped it easily around my shoulders. It made me smile, remembering that same chivalry from that night in college. He had lent me his jacket then as well, and there was no expectation there. He was just a good guy.

It made me wonder why I hadn't told him about Ronny. She could use such a gentle male influence in her life. I felt a pang of sadness and guilt, but I knew I couldn't tell him about our daughter now.

We were walking past a speakeasy that I used to love on the rare nights out with coworkers. I had never stayed for long then, but tonight, I didn't have to hurry home to Ronny.

"Come on," I said, grabbing Wes's arm and drawing him toward the door. Fortunately, the password was still the same, and we tumbled inside laughing.

"We definitely don't have anything like this in Nebraska," Wes said, looking around at the antique decorations.

I laughed. "That you know of," I said teasingly. "Let's get a drink. They do amazing cocktails."

Again, I knew I was playing with fire, but shouldn't I just enjoy this for as long as I could? Where was the harm, really?

We placed our drink orders and brought them over to a little table, standing there and sipping at them as we looked around the place. I couldn't help the swaying of my hips. The jazz band that evening was on point, one of the better acts I'd heard in a while.

Wes was still staring at me, his eyes gone dark, and suddenly he set his drink down forcefully, as though he had reached some decision after an internal battle. "Would you like to dance?" he asked, his voice husky.

I stared at him in surprise. All he had asked was if I wanted to dance, nothing more, but I could feel my heart rate quicken. "Sure," I said, unable to help the shyness that crept into my tone.

Wes captured my hand and all but dragged me out onto the dance floor. As he whirled me around, I felt even more surprised at what a good dancer he was. We flowed together,

Wes's body moving at least as smoothly and sexily as it did in bed. Or in his office, with me up on his desk.

I could feel myself getting turned on, and as the band switched to a slow and sensual song, I couldn't help wrapping my arms around him and holding him close. We moved easily through the room, and I found myself holding my breath. The moment was as fragile as spun glass, and I would do anything to make it last.

It was bound to shatter, but I tried not to think about that now. I tried to focus on every sensation, knowing I would be replaying this back over and over again in my mind for the rest of my life.

This right here was about the best I had ever felt, second only to the way I had felt the first time I held Ronny in my arms. I looked up at Wes, meeting his gaze. I knew this was wrong, but I couldn't tear myself away.

CHAPTER 11

WES

We probably shouldn't be doing this. I knew that, but I couldn't seem to stop it once things were set in motion. I hadn't been able to protest when Rian dragged me in here. And how was I supposed to stop myself when I saw the way she was moving her hips, swaying to the music?

Maybe it was the wine talking, but she was the most enchanting thing I had ever seen.

Now, with her body pressed up against mine, I wouldn't have been able to pull away if I had wanted to. The way she moved was hypnotic, and all I could think of was fucking her again. I knew I couldn't, but that just made me want to all the more.

We danced until we were breathless. I knew the sensible thing to do would be to call it a night, to go back to our hotel and ensconce ourselves in our separate rooms. Pretend like there wasn't this magnetic energy between the two of us.

At the same time, I was reluctant for the night to end. "Why don't I grab us another round?" I heard myself saying, and from Rian's all-too-eager nod, I could tell she felt the same way as me. She wanted to be here with me. Dressed in that sexy backless dress, her cheeks flushed from exertion. God. I couldn't possibly want her more.

I went to the bar to grab the drinks while she went back to the table we had stood at before. I glanced back over my shoulder at her while I was waiting for our drinks to be ready. I frowned when I noticed some guy there talking to her. She was shaking her head, her whole body leaning away from the guy in a clear sign of disinterest. The guy didn't take the hint, though.

Still, my attention was drawn back to the bartender as he set the drinks down in front of me. I paid and turned back toward Rian just in time to see the other guy grab Rian's arm and pull her toward the dance floor. The guy stumbled slightly as he did so, and I could tell he was drunk, but I wasn't about to cut him any slack on account of that. My protective instincts immediately kicked in, and I hurried over, just in time to hear Rian tell the guy that he was hurting her.

I grabbed the asshole by one shoulder and his wrist, squeezing the wrist tightly so he would let go of Rian's arm. Once the jerk's grip released, I spun him away, standing between him and Rian, glaring defiantly at him. The guy didn't take kindly to the interruption and took a swing at me, moving erratically. But drunk as he was, it was easy enough to avoid his flailing punch.

Still, the attack made me even more pissed off, and I shoved him back. Security came swooping in and grabbed both of us, hauling us toward the door while Rian yelled at them to let me go since I hadn't done anything wrong. I couldn't help but start laughing as we were pushed outside. The drunk grumbled something unkind and stumbled off. I didn't pay any attention, instead turning toward Rian as she rushed out after me.

"Are you okay?" I asked her immediately, grabbing her hand and inspecting her wrist tenderly.

"What were you laughing about?" she asked suspiciously.

I shook my head, grinning up at her. "I was just thinking that you could really use a permanent bodyguard," I teased. "Feels like I keep having to rescue you from creeps."

Rian punched my arm lightly. "Oh, shut up," she said, but that just made me laugh harder. Soon, she was laughing with me.

I smiled fondly down at her, and maybe it was the fact that I'd been turned on by her all night or maybe it was the fact that I was thinking back to that first night with her. Maybe it was the adrenaline that had rushed through me when I saw that guy grab her. Whatever it was, I suddenly just couldn't resist. I grabbed her and kissed her furiously.

Rian kissed me back, clinging to me, standing up on her tiptoes to press her mouth even tighter against mine.

The next thing I knew, we were rushing hand in hand back to the hotel, laughing as we went. Maybe it was the naughtiness of it, the fact that she and I knew better than to sleep together again, or maybe it was the fact that we fit so well with one another. Maybe it was just the wine. But somehow it felt like we were desperate schoolkids again, like the last seven years apart had never happened and like we were going at it for the first time all over again.

She pulled me into her room without giving it a moment's thought. I kicked the door closed behind us and pressed her up against it. I couldn't keep from stroking my hands down her bare back, exploring that expanse of skin which had been so tantalizing all night long. We continued to make out frantically. She mewled as I nipped at her lower lip, and the noise went straight to my groin.

I pressed a leg between her thighs, and she rocked against me, letting out a little gasp at the delicious friction.

We had been here before, twice now, but this time, even more than either of the times before, it felt like if we crossed this line, there was no going back. I hesitated for a moment, knowing that this wasn't the right thing to do but also knowing that there was no way I could stop myself. All the self-control in the world couldn't keep me from stripping her down and laying her out on those sheets. She was just too wonderful for me to ignore.

She pulled away breathlessly, and I could tell from the serious look in her eyes that she was thinking the same things as I was. "I want you," she said quietly, a certain emphasis on the words that seared them in my brain for the rest of my life. Those three words would haunt my dreams and my waking hours equally, I knew.

It was all I could do to comply with her unspoken request. I led her over to the bed and lowered her down onto it, covering her lips with mine once more.

CHAPTER 12

RIAN

I couldn't help but giggle as Wes's lips traced down along the side of my stomach, his slight stubble tickling my skin. He had already stripped me out of my dress, and we were both dressed in just our underwear on the bed. Where things between us had always verged on frantic before, this time, he seemed intent on taking his time. I wasn't complaining.

We made out until I was squirming with wet, hot lust. I had worn my sexiest semi-sheer black panties that evening, and I knew that by the time he reached them with his mouth, they would be glistening with dampness.

But he was taking his damned sweet time to get there, his tongue tracing the circles of my nipples. He licked and sucked at my breast, his dark eyes meeting mine, a teasing look to his gaze. I gasped, arching against him, but he kept his slow and steady pace, working me over until I was trembling with need and sweet lust.

He nibbled his way slowly down my body, and I arched against him, pleading with him, not even sure what it was I was asking for anymore. He tongued inside of me and I cried out, body jerking in response to the delicious sensation. He laved at my entrance, his fingers dragging sensually across my clit. Darts of pleasure tickled my lower spine, and I ached with the need for more.

When Wes finally rammed into me, his movements were slow and precise. He gave me his cock inch by slow inch, and no matter what I did, no matter how much I begged him, he wouldn't move any faster. It was delicious and excruciating and incredible all at once, the way my body reacted to his, the way it begged for more. I had never felt like this with anyone else, that was for sure.

I sobbed as I came, my whole body convulsing with pleasure, my vision going white. But Wes didn't stop there, didn't release me. Instead, he continued to thrust into me, chasing his own release. It was all I could do to lie there, to cling to him, to remember how to breathe.

I spilled again a second time as he gave one final, rough thrust into me. We collapsed together bonelessly on the sheets, both panting with exertion. I quivered with the aftershocks for a long time, barely able to string together a thought, let alone speak.

I didn't know what it was that made the sex with Wes so damned good. It had never been like this with anyone else. Was it the feelings I had for him? The fact that he was the father of Ronny and thus somehow linked to me, albeit in ways he didn't know? I wasn't sure, but I knew that as I lay there in his arms, I felt more content than I had in ages.

I liked him, that was the thing. He was a wonderful man. Caring, smart, successful. I had always known him to be driven, back when we were in college together, but there was something more now. There was a maturity to him that had been lacking then, and a certain self-confidence. It was clear he knew what he wanted out of life, and that he wouldn't let anything stop him from getting it. That was sexy. Undeniably.

He was everything I could have wanted in a man, the whole package. Unfortunately, I knew that he could never be mine. I had a huge secret, one I had been keeping from him for seven years now. If he ever found out about Ronny, everything between us would change.

I rolled over, looking up at him. His eyes were closed, but as I shifted, his hand lightly stroked my lower back, soothing me. Suddenly, I wanted to tell him everything. Surely telling him about Ronny would only draw us closer together? For one brief second, I allowed myself to imagine what it would be like to be a family, the three of us.

Except that that was nothing more than wishful thinking and naivete. There was no way that Wes would just accept the fact that he had a daughter and that I had lied to him for all of these years. Best-case scenario, he would be pissed at me for keeping her from him for all this time. Worst-case scenario, he would want nothing to do with either one of us anymore. Which, oh yeah, would be a little awkward since at the end of the day, he was still my boss.

At least for now. At least until he found out about my secret and fired me for it. I wasn't sure that it was legal for him to fire me for something like this. Would that count as an HR violation? But then again, I should have been up-front when I was hired about the fact that I had a child. Moreover, we both knew I wouldn't have the guts to sue him for firing me without a good cause. I just couldn't.

I sighed and snuggled closer. I was well aware of the fact that there was another, even more selfish reason that I didn't really want to tell him about Ronny right now. I didn't want to give this up, not yet. I liked where we were at right now, and I wasn't ready for things to change.

I wanted this: to fall into bed with him, to be fucked within an inch of my life, to curl up in his arms afterward with his talented fingers stroking aimless patterns across my skin, sending little renewed prickles of lust through my body.

Still, even as I lay there, I had to face the reality of the situation. There was no way I could continue working with Wes forever without him finding out about Ronny. Nebraska was too small of a place; it was a wonder it had taken this long for him to find out about her. He was bound to see her somewhere, or else I was bound to slip up, the way I had with Angie. Not only that, but things were only going to get more difficult the longer I kept things a secret.

No, I had to tell him about her. Not right now, but soon.

It was scary to think about it. I had no way of knowing what he might do when he found out. I didn't want Ronny to have to face the uncertainty of possibly moving again. I knew she was finally starting to feel like she had friends here, and I didn't want to tear her away from another place, and especially not when she was just starting to feel comfortable here. That wasn't the life I wanted for her.

But what could I do? I couldn't go back to the past and tell him about Ronny back when I first found out that I was pregnant with her, or back when she was first born. Nor could I go back to when I was fired from my previous job and find work anywhere else other than Nebraska. Things were the way they were. And it was about time I took responsibility for my actions.

I felt conflicted, and most of all, sad. As though sensing my emotional disturbance, Wes pulled me a little closer, holding me tightly. He lightly kissed my temple. I sighed, feeling all the angst go out of me. I just couldn't help feeling safe and secure with him, as though everything was going to be all right.

I drifted off to sleep, wishing that the feeling could last forever.

CHAPTER 13

WES

I tried to focus all my attention and energy on what we were here to do today, rather than on what had happened the night before, but it was difficult to do with Rian sitting not two feet away from me there in Devin's investment firm's boardroom. The room was palatial and well-appointed, and Devin was clearly in his element there.

My thoughts kept drifting back to that morning, though.

Waking up alone had made something ache inside of me. I shouldn't have expected that Rian would stay the night, but I guess there was a part of me that had let myself believe that if I fell asleep holding her in my arms, then I would wake up to the same luxurious feeling.

I had known something was wrong almost the minute we came down from our high, though. I had felt the way Rian stiffened in my arms. I had seen the look on her face as she looked up at me. There was something she was fighting with, some internal monster she didn't want to tell me about. Instead of asking, I had wanted to bask in the moment, resolving that I would talk to her the next day.

We had plenty to talk about, after all, and we were both

tired right then. Besides, we had been drinking. Better to come back to it the next day.

Except that in my head, we had come back to things first thing in the morning, before our meeting with Devin. Only that hadn't happened. I had woken up, and Rian was gone. I wondered if she was still thinking back to the last time we had slept together, when I'd told her it was a mistake for us to sleep together. Maybe she just didn't want to give me the chance to say anything like that again.

Or maybe this was just what she did: had sex and then disappeared. I was starting to notice a pattern here.

Either way, I'd wanted to talk to her about it, but before I could, it was time to head to breakfast with Devin before heading here so that we could do our pitch meeting. It felt like there was an elephant in the room with us as well, but I was trying to ignore that and focus.

When it was time for us to make our pitch, I found that was surprisingly easy to do—like falling back into an old habit. It helped to have Rian there with me for the pitch. She brought a sense of calm even when she had turned my whole world upside down.

I gave the introduction and an overview of the company. Then, I turned the floor over to Rian. She looked surprised when I did so, but I intended to do things just the same way we had when we were pitching to Devin. After all, this pitch was hers. She had passion and she had intelligence, and there was a reason we had her as our innovations manager.

I had to admit, I was more and more impressed as I watched her. She was nailing the pitch, and I could tell she was engaging the board members. Just like Devin had wanted, she was forging a personal connection between herself, our company, and the product line. At the end of the pitch, there was even a scattered burst of applause.

Rian looked slightly embarrassed, and I couldn't help but

put a hand on her shoulder to give her support. I had to admit I was proud of her—and even more so when the board put the matter to an immediate vote and decided to put up the investment capital.

Afterward, we all headed back to Devin's office to talk over a few of the details.

"I'm glad the board voted our way," he said, grinning at us. He turned to face Rian specifically. "Then again, how could they not with a pitch like that? I think half of them were ready to sign over their firstborns to you at the end of the pitch."

Rian laughed. "I'm not sure I would go that far," she protested.

"Well, I would," Devin said confidently. He grinned and put his arm around Rian. "You'd better get used to trusting what I say. After all, we're going to be working together pretty closely moving forward."

I stared at the two of them. Rian was smiling at Devin, and she looked far from uncomfortable with the man's overt affection. I was hit with a bout of jealousy so strong that it was like a body blow. I tried to push the feeling away. Devin was my friend, and putting his arm around Rian's shoulders was nothing more than a friendly gesture. It was just the same as when I had put my hand on her shoulder during the pitch meeting. It didn't mean anything more than that she had our support.

Still, the jealousy thing was a little worrisome. How attached was I already? Rian and I might have slept together, but at the end of the day, we were coworkers and there couldn't be anything more. Not only that, but she had made it clear, time and time again, that she wasn't looking for anything more. Because wasn't that what it had meant, waking up alone in bed that morning? That she wasn't interested in this being something more?

The truth was, I knew that that was for the best. We couldn't have anything more, not as long as I was her boss. But knowing that didn't make me want her any less. Knowing that didn't make me want to see her with Devin or anyone else.

I needed to keep things professional between us, even if I knew that I could no longer be objective where she was concerned. That meant pushing my jealousy aside and focusing on the project. I forced myself to ignore Devin's arm around her shoulders and tactfully turned the conversation back to all the things we needed to do before we left New York.

CHAPTER 14

RIAN

I felt like I was buzzing with how well the presentation to the board had gone. It had taken everything I had to focus on the presentation and not on the way it felt to see Wes again after the night we'd had.

I knew I probably should have stuck around that morning and talked to him about where we went from here, but I also knew just how important this presentation was and what it could mean for everyone at the company. That meant that I had to forget about my personal drama and focus instead on the pitch.

Which meant that when I woke up early, while Wes was still sleeping, and felt my brain starting to whirl through all kinds of thoughts about what this might mean, well. I knew I had to get out of there. So I had slipped out before he woke up.

I wasn't sure if that had been the right decision to make. I was scared that if I stuck around, though, something would be said that would distract me from the pitch. Either Wes and I would agree that we were going to continue seeing one another... or not. Either way would throw me off my game. I was equally worried about the whole Ronny thing—either I told Wes about her or I didn't. And again, either way, it was going to throw me off my game.

So I couldn't think about it. Apparently not thinking about it had worked, because we had walked out of there with the assurance from the board that they would invest in the product line. Wes and I had chatted with Devin about the next steps, and I was excited for how things were going to go.

Except that then we had left Devin's office, and now we were at lunch. Alone. Just me and Wes, and the weight of everything we had left unsaid. I wondered if I should be surprised at the fact that he hadn't said anything about the previous night. After all, he had been the one who called things a mistake last time. Maybe this time, he had decided that we just wouldn't talk about it.

I stared down at my menu, trying to think of something to say, and wondering if I had messed things up by sneaking out of there that morning. How did I explain to him that I just needed to focus on work for a moment, but I still wanted to talk things through? The only thing that came to mind was to tell him about Ronny, but if I led with that, I knew that things were sure to go badly for us.

I was surprised at how nervous I was to get things right with him. But then again, I knew he was a great man, that I loved spending time with him, that I had never felt this comfortable around any other man in my life. I didn't want to mess things up.

Especially not since now I was thinking about how if I messed things up with him, things could be messed up for Ronny, too. He was her dad, and even though seven years ago I had made the decision not to tell Wes about her, I realized now that if I continued along that vein, she would never have a *dad* in her life.

And what a great dad Wes would be, if I only let him know that his daughter existed. I felt that down to the very depths of my soul.

"By the way, if I haven't said it already, you did an amazing job with the presentation earlier," Wes said suddenly.

I smiled at him. "Thanks," I said, my nervousness creeping into my tone. Wes frowned, and I could tell he was about to say something else. Remembering how things had gone last time, I knew that I needed to speak first.

"Listen, I was thinking about last night," I said. To be honest, I still didn't even know what I was about to say to him, but whatever I said, I knew that it would be the truth.

Except that before I had a chance to say anything else to him, my phone rang. I jumped a little, staring down at the screen uncomprehendingly for a moment. Whatever train of thought I'd had scattered the rest of the way when I saw that it was Angie who was calling me. Not only that, but I saw that I had notifications. I'd had my phone on silent during the meeting, and I must not have realized that she had called me before. Then, I had been so wrapped up in the victory that again, I hadn't been paying attention.

I knew that for her to have called me more than once, though, she wasn't just checking in. Something must be wrong.

The same as when the school had called me about her, I felt my blood run cold. I knew that I couldn't blame myself, but right then and there, I suddenly wondered if I was a terrible parent. It felt like things kept happening to my daughter, and I was never there for her when they did. Now, I was halfway across the country, and who knew what had happened to her.

"I have to get this," I said to Wes, my voice barely audible to myself over the pounding of blood in my ears.

"Is everything okay?" he asked, but I didn't respond as I stood up and headed outside to the curb to answer the call with a little privacy.

"Angie, what happened?" I asked immediately, not wasting time on pleasantries.

"I feel terrible," Angie said, her voice strained. "Ronny was playing with the boys and slipped on a toy car and fell down the stairs." I could tell that she had been crying, and I felt bad, knowing logically that none of it was her fault. I didn't have it in me to console her then, though. I had to know the rest of it.

"How bad is it?" I asked, my voice barely above a whisper. I almost didn't want to know the answer to the question. It had to be bad if Angie was calling me frantically about it. But how bad?

"She's in the hospital," Angie said, and I felt like I was drowning. "She broke her arm, and the doctors are still taking care of her. They said something about the possibility of a fat embolism triggered by the broken bone? I don't know, I'm not a doctor."

She was babbling, but I couldn't get the words out to stop her. My whole world felt like it was crashing down around me. Ronny was hurt, in the hospital, and I wasn't there with her. God, she must be so scared, and Mommy wasn't *there* for her. Why the hell was I here? Who was I trying to kid? I couldn't just focus on myself and on my budding relationship with Wes; I had a daughter, and Ronny should always come first.

The moment that Devin suggested that we come with him to New York, I should have admitted to the fact that I had a daughter and that I couldn't leave her. I should have...

None of that mattered now. What was done was done. The only thing to do was get back to Nebraska as soon as possible. "I'll be there as quickly as I can," I told Angie, the words faint. I hung up and realized as I did so that my hands were shaking. I felt like I might faint, but I knew I couldn't. I needed to do something. I needed to get back to Nebraska.

Wes was there in front of me on the sidewalk, I realized, a look of concern on his face. I slowly focused on him, licking my dry lips. "I have to get back to Nebraska. Now," I told him.

"What's wrong?" Wes asked. "What happened?"

I stared at him, wondering what to say. This absolutely wasn't the way I had planned to tell him about his daughter, but how else could I explain things to him? There were no excuses that would cover something like this.

"Ronny, my daughter, had an accident. She's in the hospital," I said. I realized the second after I said it that by saying "my daughter," I had subconsciously covered the fact that she was his daughter as well. We could deal with that another time, though.

Wes was frowning at me. "I didn't know you had a daughter," he said, a hint of reproach in his tone.

I felt tears prick the corners of my eyes. Really? Did he have to be like that *now*? Now, when I had just told him that my daughter was in the hospital, he wanted to split hairs about the fact that he didn't know I was a mom?

I knew I wasn't being fair to him, though. I would have felt the same way in his situation. I would have been asking the same sorts of questions. I was only lashing out at him now because I felt bad about the whole situation and because I was desperately afraid for our daughter. Our daughter that he didn't even know about.

I closed my eyes for a moment and took a deep, if shaky, breath. "It just hasn't come up before," I finally said to Wes. It was only a lie if I looked too closely at the details.

I could tell that he wanted to say something else about it, but he seemed to realize that now wasn't the time. Instead, he pulled out his phone. "Devin?" he said when the other person picked up. I couldn't begin to fathom why he might be calling Devin. I wasn't about to think about work things right now. I needed to get back to Nebraska.

But Wes continued. "Can we use your jet right away?" he asked. "We need to get back to Nebraska. I'm afraid it's an emergency."

I couldn't hear Devin's response, but from the way Wes was nodding, I had a feeling it was an affirmative. Thank God. Wes started steering me back toward the hotel while he talked, and I let myself be led along even though there was a part of me that wanted to protest that we could just leave our things there.

I wanted to be in Nebraska *now*; I didn't want to waste time packing. I knew logically, though, that she was in good hands with the doctors and that my being there ten minutes sooner that I might have been without the trip back to the hotel wasn't what would make the difference.

I never should have been there in New York in the first place.

It was another thing I knew I shouldn't be beating myself up about. After all, I couldn't protect Ronny from everything. She was bound to get hurt at some point. I knew that kids broke bones, and it was only a matter of time before something like this happened. Besides, I had done the best thing that I could do, in placing her with Angie for the time I was gone.

I absolutely didn't blame Angie for what had happened. The same thing might have happened while I was the one looking out for Ronny.

Still, logic didn't keep me from feeling horribly guilty. Logic didn't keep me from feeling like I had failed at my task of being a mother. Logic didn't keep me from feeling like I had been way too selfish lately, first uprooting my daughter and then jetting off on a business trip without a backward glance. Maybe this was what I got for all the stupid, self-motivated things I had done lately.

I tried to push those thoughts out of my head for now, though. The quicker we were packed, the sooner we'd be on our way and the quicker I'd see Ronny again.

I stuffed my things in my bag in record time and was relieved to see Wes move just as quickly. We headed to the airport without another word. I wondered if he was mad at me for keeping from him the fact that I had a daughter. I hadn't revealed that Ronny was his, but I had revealed that I had been lying to him.

I tried to think of how I would feel if the tables were turned, but it was hard to think outside of the present. God, Ronny was in the hospital. Knowing that was the worst feeling in my whole life.

On the way to the airport, though, Wes slipped his arm around my shoulders. I still felt guilty, but I felt a little calmer about the situation. I took a deep breath. Everything was going to be all right. Somehow.

I closed my eyes and leaned into him, trying not to think about what might happen at the hospital. I knew I had to keep Wes from coming in there with me. First of all, Angie knew he was Ronny's dad, and even though she had promised to keep things a secret, I knew if we rushed in there together, she would assume I had told him.

I also knew there would be no hiding the truth from him there. Ronny had his eyes. More than that, she was the right age to be his, and he was sure to realize that. Wes was a smart guy; something like that wouldn't escape his notice.

I swallowed hard. No, he couldn't come in there with me. I had enough on my plate right now without having to deal with that on top of the other drama of Ronny being hurt. Not to mention the fact that my daughter had been through enough without having to deal with that on top of the rest of it.

For a moment, I let myself picture that alternate universe again, though. The one where we were a family. What if Wes and I could rush in there like concerned parents? What if I could have his support there with me the whole way through the process of filling out paperwork and seeing her in a hospital bed for the first time ever?

I was starting to realize just how much I had given up by making the decision not to tell him about our daughter all those years ago. If I could go back now, maybe I would have done things differently. But it was too late for that, anyway.

CHAPTER 15

WES

There was so much that I wanted to say to Rian, but I knew that now wasn't the time to get into an argument with her, and I was afraid that that was what would result right now.

I had never seen someone so upset before. Having never had a child of my own, I couldn't begin to imagine what she must feel like knowing that her daughter was in the hospital. In spite of the fact that I felt betrayed, finding out that she had kept such a huge secret from me, I wanted nothing more than to be there for her. The trouble was, I didn't know the first thing about how to be there for her in this situation. I settled for wrapping an arm around her shoulders, hoping that was somehow enough.

On the plane, she stared listlessly out the window. I would give anything to know what was going through her head right then, but I didn't know how to ask.

I found myself thinking about how I felt about all of this. I was shocked to find out she had a baby, but at the same time, I was realizing that I shouldn't be. Her body bore the marks of having had a kid, but I had overlooked them because, I guess, I had been so certain that...

That what? I didn't even know. I knew, of course, that she couldn't have been celibate since the last time we were together. Neither of us had been pining for the other. It wasn't like we had made any plans to see one another ever again. We had only happened to end up working together and rekindled what we'd had in that one night at the end of college.

It made sense that she had been with someone else. In fact, that sort of explained why she had left New York. A messy breakup, maybe a guy who meant trouble for her and her daughter. She would of course seek solace by returning to her roots in Nebraska.

Or something. Jeez, it was none of my business either way. No use speculating about it.

Except that there was part of me that felt as though it was, in fact, my business. After all, she and I had been sleeping together. More than that, I was her boss. I should have known that she had a daughter. We might have done things different with the whole New York trip.

Oh. Because, of course, that was the reason she had been so hesitant to come to New York in the first place. I felt like an ass for not realizing, even though there was no way I could have known without her telling me.

Again, my frustration started to bubble to the surface. Why hadn't she told me? Had she thought it would change things between us? Or had she been afraid that she wouldn't keep her job if we knew she had a kid? What decade did she think we were living in? I wouldn't have fired her just because she had a kid. There were plenty of successful businesswomen out there who had children.

I wanted to give her the benefit of the doubt and believe it was just that she hadn't thought it was relevant information.

That she was telling the truth when she said she hadn't told me about her daughter because it just hadn't come up. At the same time, it just seemed like it was one of those things that she might have mentioned at some point.

It was a lot to think about, but again, there was no getting into something with her now when she was already so upset. We were both likely to say things we didn't mean.

I wondered if this changed things between us, though. She would understandably be hesitant to start things with me if she was just getting out of a serious relationship with the father of her child. Maybe that explained why she had disappeared the other morning while I was still asleep. Except that it didn't explain why she had disappeared to New York without a word, back when college ended.

In any case, it would certainly change whatever type of future we might have. In the hypothetical world where somehow it was okay for Rian and me to be together, this opened a whole new can of worms. Was I ready to step in and be a father to someone, especially someone who wasn't my own child? Starting a relationship with Rian would be tricky enough, but starting a relationship where she had a kid? That took a certain level of commitment I wasn't sure that I was ready for, no matter how much I liked Rian.

Of course, that was all strictly hypothetical anyway. A relationship with Rian was out of the question for as long as I was her boss. Neither of us were willing to give up our careers to be with one another; that, I knew for a fact. And really, didn't that show me that my level of commitment to her wasn't enough to level with the fact that she had a child?

I glanced over at Rian one last time as we were landing, wishing I could say something to comfort her. But I couldn't imagine what she must feel like at the moment, and the words died on my lips. I looked silently away from her.

We walked through the airport mostly in silence. "Why

don't you let me drive you to the hospital?" I suggested as Rian hesitated near the taxi stand.

She gave me a surprised look, like she had almost forgotten I was there. "You don't have to," she said.

"Come on," I said, putting a hand on her shoulder and steering her toward the parking lot, where my silver sedan was waiting. I was surprised to feel her resistance. "I don't mind," I insisted. "It'll be faster this way, too, I'm sure."

"But..." Rian bit her lower lip, but she didn't seem to know what to say. Finally, she gave a terse nod. "Thanks."

"Sure," I said easily, leading the way to my parked car.

We were both silent on the way to the hospital, and I wondered if this was what she had been trying to avoid: the weight of all the things we had yet to talk about. It was taking everything I had not to pressure her to tell me why she hadn't ever mentioned her daughter before. I could tell how important her kid was to her, so why hadn't she ever told me about her?

The more I thought about it, the stranger it was. Did she really not trust me with that information?

We made it to the hospital finally. Rian was out of the car in a flash, the moment I had parked it, saying nothing more than a quick "thanks" as she raced toward the front of the hospital. I couldn't help but grin, in spite of the severity of the situation. I sat in the car for a moment, drumming my fingers against the edge of the steering wheel as I wondered what to do.

There was a part of me that wanted to follow her in there. I didn't want her to think that the only reason I was doing that was because I wanted to confront her about all of this right now. I genuinely cared about her, and although I knew she was mostly just worried about her daughter, I couldn't help but be worried about Rian as well. She had looked so *scared*.

Was I welcome in there, though? Was there some other reason Rian hadn't told me about her baby girl? Suddenly, another scenario popped into my head. Maybe the reason Rian hadn't told me about her daughter was that she hadn't actually just gotten out of a bad relationship prior to moving back to Nebraska. Maybe she was still together with the girl's father.

After all, someone had been caring for the girl while Rian and I were in New York over the weekend.

Would Rian really do that to me, though? She didn't strike me as the kind of person to cheat on someone. I didn't think that she and I would have had sex if there had been someone else in the picture for her. But then again, I wouldn't have expected her to have a mystery daughter either.

I shook my head. I wasn't going to be able to focus on anything else for the rest of the day anyway, not until I knew that Rian, and her daughter, were okay. Might as well make myself useful.

When I returned to the hospital, I had about a half dozen different things for lunch, plus chocolate, plus a little stuffed animal for Rian's daughter. I asked the nurse on duty where I could find Rian, and she looked like she was trying not to laugh. I guess I did go a little overboard, but I wanted Rian to know that I still cared for her, even if she had been keeping this secret from me.

I was surprised to see Angie sitting outside the room when I got there. "What are you doing here?" I asked, even more shocked to see the remnants of tears on her cheeks.

She looked up at me and winced. "I was watching Ronny for Rian while she was in New York," she explained. "Ronny was playing with my boys, and that's how she got hurt. She fell down the stairs."

I blinked in surprise. So Angie had known about Rian's daughter when I hadn't? Again, I couldn't help but feel betrayed by Rian's secret. Why had she kept it from me? And why hadn't Angie ever said anything about it? I had to assume that Rian had asked her not to, since Angie was usually an open book. But why would she ask her not to tell me, and why would Angie agree?

None of this made any sense. I knew that Angie wasn't the one I should be hounding for answers, though. Fortunately, before I could say anything dumb, Angie noticed the bags in my hands.

"Is that food?" she asked in surprise.

"Yeah," I said, feeling a bit sheepish as I held up the bags. God, it looked like I was preparing to feed an army. "I didn't know what Rian might want, but I figured she might be hungry. We were in the middle of getting lunch when she got the phone call to come back here."

"That's really nice of you," Angie said, and from the way she looked at me, brow furrowed, I wondered if she suspected something. I must be overreacting, though. She might have known about Rian's daughter, but surely Rian hadn't told her about *us*.

"You hungry?" I asked, sitting down next to Angie.

"Starving," she admitted.

I held out the bags to her, letting her pick what she wanted. "How's... Ronny anyway?" I asked, glancing toward the room.

"She's not in there right now," Angie said just as I started thinking of barging in there. Whether Rian wanted me there or not. I turned my gaze back toward Rian's assistant. "They took her in for surgery. Rian went with them, although I doubt she'll be allowed in the lab during the procedure." She shook her head, looking mournful. "I still can't believe this happened."

"I'm sure it wasn't your fault," I said, carefully sitting down next to her. "Kids will be kids and all of that." It sounded lame as the words came out of my mouth, but I didn't know what else I could say to her. I barely knew the first thing about parenting. Undoubtedly Angie, who had three boys of her own, knew it wasn't her fault, and my empty platitudes weren't going to make her feel any better.

Yet again, I found myself wondering what the hell I was doing there. After all, Rian clearly didn't want me around her daughter, for one reason or another. I was intruding by being there. I should go home or maybe try to go in to the office to get some work done. There were still some things to be ironed out with the new product line, and if I could video conference with Devin, maybe I could have things all ready to go by the time Rian was ready to get back to work.

Not that I had any idea when that might be. She would probably be even more protective of her daughter from here on out, and I wouldn't be able to blame her for that. I wondered if she was going to be able to stay as the lead on this project. She definitely deserved it, with the pitch she had given—and god, was that only this morning? It felt like forever ago now.

Whether Rian deserved to be lead on the project or not, though, I couldn't blame her if her attention was turned else-where for the foreseeable future. As much as I hated the thought of losing her talents at the company so soon, I wouldn't be able to hold it against her if she had other things on her mind.

I had just gotten to my feet, thinking that maybe it would be better for me to leave, when a nurse wheeled a gurney down the hallway. I automatically stepped back to let her past, my eyes drawn to Rian on the far side of the bed. She looked pale but determined, and there was a small smile on her face. She was holding hands with the little girl in the bed, and I could tell she was damned proud of her baby girl. And that she was exhausted.

I took all of that in a moment's glance. Then, my eyes fell to the little girl's face. She was older than I had expected her to be, but that wasn't what made my blood run cold. She was the spitting image of her mother, except for the eyes. Those eyes...

I shook my head to clear it of the image of those orbs which looked so similar to my own. No way. As she was wheeled into the room, Rian following after her, I felt rooted to my spot. Those eyes were so much like mine. And although I didn't know too much about kids, I would swear that the girl was maybe six or so. Rian must have had her right after college.

It couldn't be a coincidence, could it?

My heart was hammering in my chest, my body hit by a wave of emotion. Shock, anger, confusion—I didn't even fully know what I was feeling anymore. This was worse than the betrayal I'd felt when Rian revealed she had a daughter she had never told me about. That had been a big enough secret, on its own. But this?

Was it possible the girl was my daughter? Was that the reason why Rian had never told me about her? My hands clenched into fists at my sides as I fought to control myself. If I went in there shouting now, there was no way she would ever let me near the girl again, whether I was her father or not. Nor did I want to scare that little girl whose eyes were so much like my own.

I needed answers, though.

I looked at Angie, wondering if she knew. Something in her eyes assured me that she did. The thought made me feel sick. What the hell kind of man did Rian think I was, that she didn't even want to admit to me I had fathered a child with her? Did she think I'd be such a terrible influence on the girl?

All my logic went out the window. I stalked into the room

and scowled at Rian. "We need to talk," I said, my voice low and level but seething with anger.

She paled even further, if that was possible. I no longer felt concern for her, though, my own feelings taking precedence over my worry for her.

CHAPTER 16

RIAN

I had been relieved when Wes didn't follow me into the hospital. I hadn't even had to think up some kind of excuse to get him out of there; he had just left. Of course, there was a part of me that ached at the fact that he hadn't even tried to stick around. I mean, it wasn't like we were in a relationship. I had been the one to rush out of there that morning before we had any sort of talk about what had happened last night.

Still, I guess I had thought that his tenderness the night before meant he cared for me. Or if not that, then at least the way he had quickly found a way to get us back to Nebraska, not to mention the fact that he had offered to drive me to the hospital.

I couldn't dwell on all of that, though. I raced into the hospital and found out where Ronny was. When I got to her room, she was asleep in her bed, looking small and fragile and pale, and I immediately started sobbing. Angie had been there to hug me and tell me that everything was going to be all right.

Just when I had finally started to calm down, the doctor

had come in and informed me that they were taking Ronny in for surgery to fix her broken arm and make sure there was nothing worse going on in there that they hadn't seen in the X-ray. I nearly fainted at the thought of it: my little girl going in for surgery.

Immediately, I wished Wes was there with me. He might not know that Ronny was his, and now wasn't the time to tell him, but his strength would have been so wanted just then. Damn the consequences.

Of course, now that he was here again, inexplicably back at the hospital and sitting beside Angie, I wished I had never hoped for his presence there. I could see from the look in his eyes that he had put two and two together. That he knew that Ronny must be his.

What could I do? Lying about it wouldn't help the situation, and besides, he would never believe me. The gig was up. I had no choice but to admit that she was his.

I felt so tired right then that it was a wonder I stayed standing. As I faced the anger and hurt in Wes's eyes, I wished that I were anywhere else. Or that somehow I had found the strength to tell him about her before now. Who had I thought I was kidding? There was no keeping something like this a secret forever, especially not once I found out that he was going to be my new boss.

I swallowed hard, barely able to continue to meet Wes's eyes. I was just glad that Ronny was asleep now, worn-out from all the drama and woozy from the painkillers they had her on. Still, I didn't want to have this conversation here.

Fortunately, Angie walked in just then. "Wes, you know now isn't the time," she said quietly.

Wes looked at her as though he didn't even know her. His frown deepened. "I think this is between me and Rian," he said, his tone icy. He turned his glare back on me. "In spite of the fact that you seem to think you can keep me out of all of it."

I winced, looking down for a moment at my baby girl. I automatically reached out to smooth her hair back, my hand resting gently on her forehead for a moment. She barely stirred, and I sighed.

I turned back to Wes. "I owe you an explanation," I said slowly.

"A couple of them, maybe," he said snidely.

I nodded, acceding the point. "You're right," I said. "But I can't do this right now. Not here, and not right now. Please. I promise I'll tell you everything later, but right now, I just need to be alone with my daughter."

Wes's face hardened. "Our daughter," he corrected. "I'm right, aren't I? She's mine?"

I looked down at Ronny again. Asleep, she looked so much like me. Unless you knew what you were looking for: that little dimple in her left cheek, the shape of her fingers. Awake, her eyes were a dead giveaway. It was what I had been afraid of all along: that as soon as Wes saw her, he would realize she was his.

Well, he had realized it. What was I going to do but admit to it?

I nodded. "She's yours," I said softly. I looked up again, my breath catching in my throat. "Please, I can't do this right now."

Maybe that was selfish of me, but I couldn't help it. The whole day had been such an emotional roller coaster already, and the last thing I wanted was to have it out with him here. I just wanted to collapse into a seat next to Ronny's bed, watching over her as she slept, reassuring myself she was going to be okay.

It was the first time I had ever had to see my baby in the hospital, and if I had thought it was bad when she was sick, it was nothing compared to this. Added to the guilt of not having been there when she was hurt, I felt guilty that I only understood about half of what the doctors were saying about her. Fat embolisms and fractured ulnas and who knew what else. I was totally out of my depth, and I was terrified that if I misunderstood something, then somehow she was never going to get 100 percent better.

Here she was, the best gift that the world had ever given me, and she was hurt and lying broken in a hospital bed. I felt sick and like I was on the verge of a meltdown, and Wes's anger wasn't doing anything to help me. Especially not since I knew that his anger was justified. I would have been just as upset if the situations were reversed.

I knew that by all rights he probably should be allowed to stay there and reassure himself that his daughter was all right, too. At the same time, he didn't have the bond I had with Ronny. He hadn't given birth to her, and he hadn't watched her grow up. That might be through no fault of his own, but at that moment, I needed him out of there. I couldn't deal with any more drama right now.

Wes's face hardened with anger. "Fine," he said, turning on his heel and stalking out of there.

I collapsed into a chair, tears starting. I had never felt so helpless in my life. My baby girl was lying in a hospital bed, and the man I had feelings for had found out my lies and probably never wanted to see me again.

Angie sighed and came over to give me another hug. She had been wonderful through all of this, and even though I knew she felt guilty about what had happened, I also knew that I could never blame her for it.

I clung to her for a while, until all my tears were gone again. Angie shook her head. "She's going to be all right," she said softly. "She's just as much of a tough little fighter as her mama."

I managed a watery smile at that. "Thanks," I said.

"Wes left some food," Angie added. "I have to get back to the boys, but why don't I bring it in for you?"

I nodded, surprised to hear that Wes had brought food. I was even more surprised with the amount of food that Angie brought in. She grinned at me. "If I didn't know better, I'd say that he was worried about you," she said, winking at me.

Suddenly, I felt even more guilty about the fact I hadn't told him about our daughter. Here I'd thought that he had just left me there at the hospital and disappeared, when in reality he'd gone out to get food for me. He was a better man than I deserved.

Angie carefully set a small stuffed deer on the bed next to Ronny. I frowned quizzically at her. "Where did that come from?" I asked. I had never seen it in my life.

Angie grinned. "Wes brought that, too," he said.

"A deer?" I asked, examining the thing, trying to figure out what it represented. The only thing that came to mind was Bambi...

"Nebraska's state animal," Angie said helpfully. She winked. "I think maybe he wanted Ronny to know that she's welcome here?" She left me to puzzle over that on my own.

I sighed as I stared at the bags of food. I was hungry, I had to admit. I hadn't even realized I was hungry, in fact, until the food was in front of me, but now it felt like I could eat it all. I pulled out a container of brisket and mac-n-cheese from a nearby BBQ place. Comfort food was just what I needed right then.

Unfortunately, eating didn't do anything to make me feel less guilty. Between not being there for Ronny and never telling Wes about our daughter, I felt like an absolute dirtbag. What's worse was that I didn't know what would happen next. Would I have to move away with Ronny again? Would Wes fire me over this?

If he didn't fire me, would we still be able to work together? If not, I was going to have to quit. I had to admit, I found it hard to believe we'd be able to work together anywhere near as seamlessly as we had before. There was no way he would ever be able to trust me again.

And there was no way that I could be around him for the rest of my life knowing I could never have him. I realized that up until now, I had harbored thoughts that maybe things would work out between us. Even though he was my boss and seemed intent on not letting anything more develop between us, I'd been sure that things would work out in the end.

Right now, though, everything felt doomed. How could I ever win him back? I looked down at Ronny, lying prone in the bed. This broken arm might not be wholly my fault, but it was my fault she didn't know who her dad was, that he had never been a part of her life. Her dad was a wonderful man, the kind of guy who brought food to the hospital without being asked, even when things weren't fully right between us.

I had denied her that relationship, and that made me feel even more terrible than all the rest of it. What kind of mother was I?

I pushed the food to the side and started crying again.

CHAPTER 17

WES

I had barely slept last night. I couldn't seem to stop tossing and turning, wondering how the hell Rian could have kept such a huge secret from me. Was it really possible that I had a daughter? How had I never even suspected it? Shouldn't I have somehow known?

I kept thinking back to that night in college. The details of it had always been so clear to me, but thinking back now, I couldn't for the life of me remember if we had used protection. Had the condom broken? I had no idea. I felt guilty for having put Rian into that situation, even though clearly it hadn't slowed her down one bit.

I couldn't help but smile proudly as I thought of that. I hadn't seen much of her as a mother just yet, but I had to admit that I had liked what I had seen. There had been a fierce protectiveness in her eyes, and a sure faith that her daughter could do anything.

I bet she was just as amazing a mother as she was a businesswoman. I wondered why I had never picked up on those traits in her before.

Even though Rian had admitted that Ronny was mine, even though the proof was right there in the way that child's eyes looked up at me for that brief moment, I couldn't help wondering if maybe I was jumping the gun a little bit. Maybe I was wrong. Maybe Rian didn't know who the father was, and it was just a coincidence that she had the same eyes as me?

That would explain the reason Rian had never told me about the girl. She didn't know for sure that I was the father, and she hadn't wanted to burden me. It seemed like a weak reason, though. How hard was it to ask for a paternity test, in this day and age?

No, the only possible explanation was that for some reason or another, Rian didn't want me to know about the baby. What did that say about her regard for me? About the kind of man she expected I was? I knew that we'd had a rough relationship in college, but that didn't mean that I wouldn't have shown up for her. It wasn't fair for her to expect me to be some kind of deadbeat dad.

If I had a daughter, she was, what, seven years old now? Seven years old, and I had just learned her name yesterday. Seven years old, and I had just learned about her existence yesterday. What would have happened if she hadn't gotten hurt while we were in New York? How long would things have gone on without Rian telling me about her?

That was the thing that bothered me the most, honestly. Rian and I had slept together a couple of times now since she had come to work for me in Nebraska, and although we hadn't promised anything to one another, she still shouldn't have kept such a huge secret from me.

I knew her reasons for not wanting to talk things through the previous day. I had seen the exhaustion on her face, and I had known that Angie was right when she reminded me that the hospital was neither the time nor the place for a conversation like that. At the same time, I hated that we had left things so unresolved.

It made for a sleepless night, and today I felt terrible— hurt, and most of all confused. How could she do this to me? To us? To our daughter? Most of all, though, I felt worried. I had a daughter, a daughter whom I had just found out about when she was brought to the hospital. I knew that broken bones were relatively commonplace for kids, but I couldn't help feeling scared. What if I lost my daughter before I ever even got a chance to know her?

It wasn't my decision not to know about her, but now that I knew about her, I wasn't going to let anything keep me from building a relationship with her, I decided. Even if that apparently wasn't what Rian wanted. I was Ronny's father, and that meant I had certain rights. I was sure of it.

I knew I should go into work. All my focus had been on the investment project and Devin's company lately, but there were other things happening at the business as well. I was the CEO of the company, and I couldn't allow myself to get distracted by personal issues. In some ways, I had more responsibility for everyone at the company than I did for my own daughter.

Logic couldn't keep me focused today, though. The next thing I knew, I was back at the hospital.

I paused outside in the parking lot, thinking through why I was here. There was definitely a part of me that wanted to confront Rian. A huge part, in fact. I had to know why she didn't tell me about the pregnancy, and why even after moving back to Nebraska she hadn't told me about the fact that she had a daughter.

I tried to think things through in my head. I didn't want to sound too mean or accusatory, but I figured I had a right to know the answers to at least some of my questions. Yesterday had no doubt been a stressful day for her, but it was a new day now. Surely we could at least talk about some of these things through?

When I went inside and saw her sitting in the waiting room, however, I knew I couldn't confront her. She looked distraught as she stared sightlessly at the magazine in her lap. There were dark circles under her eyes, and I could tell that she had slept even less than I had. My heart went out to her. I knew I had to wait for a better time and a better place, just like Angie had said the previous day.

Right now, Rian needed the support of a friend more than she needed to hear me torrent at her for lying to me. I had a feeling, based on her tired expression, that our daughter's health wasn't the only thing that had weighed on Rian's mind the night before.

I turned and headed for the cafeteria, grabbing a tray of breakfast and coffee for her. When I got back and held it out to her, she stared blankly up at me. Then, she bit her lower lip, dropping her gaze. Sure enough, she looked worn-out and guilty. "Wes," she started to say.

I sat down beside her. "We need to talk," I said, in a much gentler tone than the one I had used the previous day. At the end of the day, I was baffled by her actions and upset that she hadn't trusted me to know about the existence of our daughter, but I still cared about Rian. There was a part of me that just wanted to look out for her, to care for her, to make sure she was going to be all right.

"Not now," I clarified. "I just wanted to be here to help if you needed anything." I paused. "Is Ronny doing all right?"

Rian looked uncertain for a moment, like she was still expecting me to blow up at her. "She's doing better," she finally said. "They were doing some tests with her right now, physical therapy stuff or something. They said I could go back in after a little while."

I nodded. "Good," I said.

"If you wanted to come with me, you could," Rian added, looking shy for the first time I had ever seen.

"I'd like that," I agreed quietly. I sat back in my seat, watching semi-critically as Rian picked at the breakfast I'd brought her. "How are you doing?"

Rian sighed and wrapped her hands around the coffee, warming them. "It was a long night," she finally said. She stole a glance over at me. "I kept wishing... that you were here."

I reached out and gently squeezed her shoulder. "You should have called me," I said.

"I was afraid to," Rian admitted. "You're right, we do need to talk. I'm not sure that I handled things right. I mean, I can explain all my reasons for it, but I don't know. If I had to do it all over again, I don't know." She frowned, trying to find the words, but before she could babble anything else, one of the nurses came over to us.

"Mrs. James? I just wanted to let you know that Ronny is all done with the doctors, and you're welcome to go back in to see her again if you'd like. Your husband, too."

"Thank you," Rian said warmly, not bothering to correct her and say that I wasn't her husband. That sent a certain thrill through me. I liked the idea, I realized, of people thinking we were a family. Even if I still wasn't sure I was ready to be a dad.

I was sure that was just nerves, though, brought on by the fact that this whole thing had happened so suddenly. Most people had the better part of a year to get used to the idea that they were going to be a father. Then they spent years watching that kid grow up. I had missed all of that, and now I was facing the fact that my kid was already in school and I was just learning about her. It was a shock to the system.

I was sure I would get used to it. I wanted to get used to it. I just hoped I wouldn't have to fight Rian on it.

I glanced over at her as we headed back to Ronny's room. She happened to glance over me at the same time, her feet slowing to a stop as we neared the door. "I'll introduce you to her, but is it all right if I don't tell her that you're her father? Just for now, while she's in the hospital? She's already been through a lot, and I know it's not fair to you, but I also don't want to overburden her. The doctor said that too much stress could be bad for her right now."

I pulled Rian into a spontaneous hug. There was a part of me that didn't want to go a minute longer without Ronny knowing I was her father, but at the same time, I knew Rian was right. At the moment, I had to think about my daughter and how much of a shock it might be to her to find out who her father was.

It was the first decision I made as a parent.

Rian slumped against me for a moment, her arms wrapping tightly around my waist. Neither of us said a word, but we didn't have to. "Come on," she said softly as she pulled away. She caught my hand and led me into the hospital room.

"Mommy!" Ronny exclaimed delightedly as she saw her mother.

"There's my brave little angel," Rian said, beaming at the girl as she went over to her, giving her a big hug, mindful of the cast. She nodded approvingly. "A bright pink cast looks very good on you."

Ronny giggled. "Can you draw me a picture on it?" she asked.

"Later, I promise," Rian said. "I have to think of the perfect one first. After all, you're going to have to look at it for *weeks*."

Ronny laughed again. Her eyes focused on me, and she cocked her head to the side. "Who's that?"

Rian gestured for me to come closer. "This is my boss and

my very good friend Wes," she said. "I knew him in college, and yesterday he gave me a ride to the hospital so I could come see you."

"Oh, okay," Ronny said. "Do you want to draw a picture on my cast?"

I grinned, trying not to feel too out of my depth here. But she seemed easygoing, and Rian's grin was reassuring. "I think I'll let your mom have the first honors," I told her. I winked at Ronny. "Whatever she draws, I'll have to draw something better."

Ronny snickered. Rian rolled her eyes. "Challenge accepted," she said, and there was a certain fondness in her voice that hadn't been there before. It put me further at ease.

There was a lot we needed to talk about. And, I realized, there was a lot I needed to talk to George and our HR department about. I was going to be in this little girl's life from here on out. That meant that all the rules about boss-employee relationships were out the window. Whatever the cost, though, I was happy to pay it.

I barely knew this little bundle of energy, but I could already tell my life would never be the same again.

CHAPTER 18

RIAN

It melted my heart to see Ronny and Wes together. She still didn't know that he was her father, but she seemed to like him all the same. I couldn't help feeling enormously relieved that Wes hadn't fought me on that. When he had showed up at the hospital that morning, I had thought for sure he was there to confront me about what he had learned the previous day, and I had steeled my nerves for it even though I didn't feel like I could handle that then.

He'd been nothing but kind, though. In fact, same as the day before, he had brought me food, looking out for me while I was frantically doing my best to look out for Ronny. I couldn't tell him how much I appreciated it. It meant everything to me.

We were definitely going to have a real conversation sometime in the very near future, and I had a feeling that things were going to get emotional. But for now, things were going as good as they could go.

I wished I had a chance to think of all the things I wanted to say to Wes when we had that conversation. Last night, though, my mind had been pretty much blank. I hadn't been able to think of much of anything beyond the way that Ronny looked in that hospital bed, the way I had felt when Angie had called me in New York, and the way Wes's eyes had flashed with anger as he stormed out of there the previous day. Those three things played over and over again on a loop in my head, making it impossible for me to get any sleep.

I felt like shit today, and I wasn't sure that I could explain anything to Wes. I definitely wasn't ready to have a conversation where we discussed our daughter's future and how he would be a part of her life. At the same time, I knew it was all a conversation I had been putting off for way too long now. It was about time to come clean on everything and work toward a setup that would work for both of us.

I considered Wes as he joked with Ronny. He was good with her, I had to admit. Not that it was difficult; Ronny was the kind of kid that everyone seemed to get along with. Still, it was good to see the two of them bonding, even if we had to be in the hospital for it to happen.

Ronny fell asleep not too long after that, worn-out still from the pain and the stress of it all. I stared down at her for a long moment, Wes's arm tentatively draped around my shoulder. "I think I'm starting to understand how you feel," Wes murmured. He held up a hand before I could say anything. "I know, I know, not entirely. You're the one who got to watch her grow up. She's closer to you than anyone else in the world. I sort of understand, though."

I frowned at him, trying not to write him off immediately. I appreciated what he was trying to say, and as I thought back to how I had felt the first time I held Ronny in my arms, I knew that that bond had formed quickly. In any case, what was there to fight? He was in her life now, for better or for worse. And I had a feeling that it was all for the better.

"She looks like she's going to be out for a while," Wes said carefully. "There's a little coffee shop down the block. Why don't we go get some real coffee in you? Get you away from the pastel walls for a minute?"

I stared at him. I couldn't just leave her here. What if she woke up and her mom wasn't there? Again? On the other hand, I knew that I was getting to that point of restless exhaustion where I needed to stretch my legs a little. Ronny was sleeping soundly, her good arm wrapped around the stuffed deer that Wes had brought for her the previous day. Besides, she was in good hands here at the hospital. The worst was behind us now.

"Okay," I found myself agreeing.

Wes smiled and led me out of there. On the pavement, I stood blinking at the sunshine for a moment. My sense of time was all thrown off after a night spent trying to sleep on a hard hospital chair. The fresh air felt good on my face.

"There's a little color coming back into you," Wes said approvingly as we walked down the street.

I grinned wanly at him. "This is probably the worst thing I've ever gone through in my life," I admitted quietly. I paused and then ducked my head. "I'm glad you've been here with me through it."

"Of course," Wes said easily, not commenting on the fact that I'd seemingly done everything in my power to keep him away from this little corner of family.

What did I want, from here on out? I knew we were going to have to talk about it, and I wished I was more prepared than I was. I wasn't sure that I was ready to start calling the three of us a family just yet. For so long, it had just been me and Ronny.

Besides, it was a big commitment to bring Wes into our little bubble. Ronny had already gotten hurt once this week.

What if things with Wes weren't permanent? What if Ronny and I moved back to New York?

I doubted I could keep my position with the company, with Wes as my boss, if everyone knew that we had a kid together. That meant that Ronny and I were going to have to leave town. I would never want to set her up for a lifetime of sadness and separation, and neither did I want to set myself up for a mess of shared custody and "who gets her for the holidays."

Except... Except that I realized now just how unfair it had been for me to keep Ronny from her father for all these years. I realized that Wes was a great man who would go out of his way to make sure his daughter was being taken care of. Maybe it was about time Ronny's and my bubble expanded. After all, she was growing up; it was only a matter of time before that bubble started to get bigger through no action of my own. Why not bring a good influence into her life while I still had the chance?

"Easy over there," Wes said suddenly. I looked over at him in surprise. "You're thinking loud enough to give me a headache." He grinned, his tone teasing, but I just sighed and looked away.

"So what am I thinking about, then?" I challenged him.

"Let's get coffee first. Then we'll talk," Wes said, steering me toward the counter. "I don't think either of us slept much last night."

We placed our orders and grabbed a small table. I wondered how many of the other people in the shop were there because of the proximity to the hospital, and how many others were just going about their everyday lives. Suddenly, I ached to be back to my usual routine. I hoped Ronny was discharged soon; I didn't know how much more of this I could take.

Wes reached out across the table, covering my hand with his own, and suddenly things felt a lot more bearable.

"I think you're thinking," he said slowly, getting back to my earlier challenge, "that you're feeling guilty. That somehow you did something wrong by being in New York when all of this happened. Which is ridiculous because you're a mom but not a superhero. You can't be everywhere at once."

He paused. "Besides, what you were doing in New York, it's pretty obvious that was for her. I mean, your work is for you as well. I know that you love this kind of job. At the end of the day, though, I was wondering where all your passion came from in that pitch. Now I think I have an idea. You're doing this for her, to give her opportunities."

My shoulders slumped, the tension going out of them. It was just that easy for him to reassure me that none of this was my fault. That I had been right to go to New York.

I rubbed a hand over my tired face. The next thing I knew, I was crying.

"Hey," Wes said, sliding his chair around so that he was next to me, his knee pressed against mine and his hand lightly stroking the back of my neck. "Listen, we don't need to talk about all of this now. I know it's been a rough couple of days for you, and I just want to be here for you. We can figure the rest of it out later."

I shook my head, tears still dripping freely down my face. "I want to talk about some of it now," I said quietly. "Because if I don't, then I might never tell you the whole story." As much as I wanted to think we would talk things out later, I knew that I was at my most vulnerable now, ready to really talk about the reasons I had kept the truth from him.

Besides, not talking about all of it felt like purposefully keeping space between us right then. I didn't want that space between us. I wanted to know if he was going to be there to support me or if I was going to lose my job. I needed to have some idea of how things were going to go. I just couldn't handle another minute of not knowing.

I took a deep breath, deciding to start from the beginning. "The night you and I hooked up, I wasn't just out celebrating the end of finals," I said. "I also found out that day that I got the internship. I didn't tell you about it then because I knew how much you wanted it. I'm pretty sure the only reason they picked me over you was because I'm a girl. They were looking to hire more female employees."

Wes frowned. "All right," he said slowly. "You didn't have to disappear without saying goodbye, though."

"I did," I sighed. "Look, I enjoyed that night. Maybe too much. Not to mention the fact that I was kind of scared. Moving to New York might have been easy for you, but I was afraid I was going to be just some hick out of her element there. I was afraid that if I said goodbye, I might not go."

Wes was quiet for a moment. "I wanted that internship," he finally said. "I would have supported you going, though. I mean, sure, I probably would have been a little upset that it was you and not me who got it, but I would have supported you. I would have helped you through your worries about being just some hick."

I shrugged. "I believe you," I said. "Back then, though, it just felt like something that I had to go through on my own." I paused. "I didn't know I was pregnant until I was already in New York."

"And what, that was another thing that you just had to go through on your own?" Wes asked, but there was no bitterness in his voice. He was clearly trying to understand my decisions. I appreciated that.

Still, that didn't make explaining things any easier. I had to try, though.

"Here's why I didn't tell you," I began.

CHAPTER 19

WES

I f the previous day had been an emotional roller coaster, this one was no less of one. From wanting to confront Rian to wanting to care for her, to getting to meet my daughter for the first time, to sitting here in a coffee shop listening to Rian explain why she had never said goodbye—it was a lot. It felt good to clear the air, though. I realized I had a lot of feelings from back in college that I had pushed aside after she started working for me, and it was good to go through those now.

It had hurt to find out she had disappeared without a word. If our roles had been reversed, I didn't think I would have made the same decision as she had. On the other hand, I understood her decision, more or less.

"I had to make a decision, when I found out that I was pregnant," Rian was saying. "Of course I was going to keep it. Her." She smiled softly. "There was never really any question of that."

I thought back to Ronny, lying there in the hospital bed. It would have been so easy for her to be moody and upset. She was tired and in pain and in a foreign environment. Somehow, though, she had been happy-go-lucky and cute. I could tell she was a little ray of sunshine.

"I had a choice, though," Rian continued. "I could either let you know about the baby, forcing you to make some very tough choices, or I could keep her a secret." She paused. "We were only together for that one night, so I didn't have any idea if you'd even want to know. I didn't know if you wanted to have kids or what you pictured for your life. Meanwhile, I just kept thinking about how much having a baby could change my life and my career. I was willing to go through with that, but I didn't know if you would be."

She shook her head. "The last thing I wanted was for you to think that you had some obligation to me. I think I knew even then that you were a good guy, that you would have found a way to make things work. I didn't want you to feel like you had to move to New York, though, or like you had to take care of us."

"Wasn't that my choice to make, though?" I asked quietly. "By not telling me about it, you didn't let me decide what I wanted to do."

To be honest, I didn't know what I would have done in that situation. It would have been confusing, that was for sure. Here Rian had disappeared on me after our one night together, and right about the time that I'd started to move on with my life and tried to forget about her, she would have called me back to let me know that I was going to be a father.

Would I have moved to New York? How different would my life have been if I had? I liked where I was at now, and I wouldn't trade it for anything. At the same time, I was always going to regret the fact that I didn't get to know my daughter, or even learn of her existence, until she was seven years old.

"We can't change that now, I guess," I said slowly.

"We can't," Rian agreed. She stared down at her hands. "I

think part of it was just, it was better to assume things than to tell you and risk the fallout. I didn't want to deal with your rejection. Of me, or of Ronny."

I stared at her for a moment, then reached out and lightly stroked her cheek. She looked over at me in surprise. "Just so we're clear, I don't like your reasons for not telling me," I said sternly. "That said, I can understand them."

I really could, too. We had both been so young back then, and she was right—she couldn't have known what my plans for the future were. In fact, she probably thought that keeping me from the responsibility of having Ronny was some sort of consolation prize in return for her taking the internship I'd wanted. She had left me open to the opportunity of other job possibilities that I wouldn't have had if I had been intent on becoming a family man.

I had worked long hours back when I first started with the company, which was how George originally got to notice me. I wouldn't have been able to do all of that if I had had a daughter to come home to every evening.

"Are you going to fire me now?" Rian asked, her eyes full of worry. "I'm sorry that I didn't tell you the truth, and I know it makes things complicated, but if you fire me, I might have to move again and I don't want to do that to Ronny. She's just starting to make friends here and get all settled in."

I shook my head. "Of course I'm not going to fire you," I said. "I wish you had told me about her, but I'm not an asshole. Besides, I don't want you to have to move. I want to get to know my daughter."

Rian's eyes widened. She slowly nodded. "Maybe you could come over for dinner sometime?" she suggested shyly. "You know, once Ronny is out of the hospital?"

I wanted a lot more than just dinner. It was going to take a lot of time to make up for seven years of not knowing that my daughter existed. But for now, I would take what I could get. I was just glad that Rian seemed receptive to the idea of me spending time with Ronny. "That sounds great," I said to Rian. "If it's too much trouble, though, don't worry about cooking. We can just order something, or I'll bring something over. Whatever works."

I didn't want her to stress too much. She had a lot on her plate as it was. Then again, apparently she'd been juggling being a mom against furthering her career for all these years since college. Suddenly, her resume—which had already looked pretty damn impressive—looked even more incredible.

Rian frowned. "Aren't you supposed to be at work or something?" she said.

I groaned. "Aren't you?" I joked half-heartedly. "I couldn't go in there without knowing where we stood and making sure that you, both of you were okay."

Rian smiled sweetly, laying her hand lightly over mine, where it rested on her leg. "We're okay," she said quietly. "We're all going to be okay."

I felt a warmth flicker inside of me, but I didn't examine it too closely right then. We were going to be okay, but things at the moment were still a little shaky between us. It was going to take some time to build up trust and all of that. Still, it was a start.

"I guess I'd better get back," I sighed.

"Thanks for coming by," Rian said. "I'll let you know when Ronny is discharged, and when I can get back to work again."

"Sure," I said, leaning in to give her a quick kiss on the cheek. I didn't dare for anything more right now. The timing wasn't right. It did feel like things were going to be okay, though. Somehow.

I headed back to work in much better spirits than I had woken up with. I knew I probably had a pile of work a mile high waiting for me, but I felt like I could take on the world right then.

Beth narrowed her eyes at me as I walked in. "Where have you been?" she asked. "Devin called yesterday and asked if you had made it back all right. What's going on?"

"Just a little medical thing, nothing for you to worry about," I said to her. "I've been with Rian at the hospital. Everything is going to be all right now, though." As I walked past her to my office, I noted that she didn't look particularly thrilled by my answer.

Whatever, though. I had a feeling that Beth was jealous of Rian. Maybe she had a crush on me, or maybe it was some sort of power thing between the women. I didn't know, but I didn't particularly care for it. That said, I knew that addressing it would likely only make things worse. Besides, I had enough on my plate at the moment without dealing with schoolgirl fits of jealousy.

I headed into my office and shut the door, trying to focus on the things I had to do. As expected, there was quite a lot of it. Hell, even my emails were going to take me a lifetime to sort through.

Or maybe it only felt that way because I still couldn't stop thinking about Rian and Ronny. I was glad that things were all out in the open now and that we seemed to be on the same page, but it was definitely going to take a while to work up my trust for Rian again.

Especially with comments about how if I fired her, she was going to move. Surely she couldn't just make decisions like that without consulting me. I started to wonder again about what my rights were. Maybe I should find a lawyer and talk to them about it? How messy would that make things in the business sense?

What about telling George and HR? Should I do that now? Should I talk to Rian about that first?

Earlier, at the coffee shop and at the hospital, things had seemed so simple. Like we had resolved all of the most difficult things. Rian was willing to let me get to know our daughter, and we were going to keep working together professionally. Now, though, it seemed like there were a dozen loose threads. Pull any one of them and this whole thing would unravel.

Was this how parenthood was supposed to feel? Or did things only feel this way because Rian wasn't letting me in? The fact that she had kept Ronny a secret from me for so long still didn't sit right, even if I was trying my best to move on.

I had no idea what the future held. As much as I wanted to focus on my work, I found myself researching lawyers. I stopped short of contacting them for now, but just in case, I wanted to have a backup plan. I wasn't going to let my daughter disappear out of my life again. That just wasn't going to happen.

CHAPTER 20

RIAN

On the one hand, it felt good to be home from the hospital. Going to sleep in my own bed felt like a miracle, and the food was exponentially better, too. Besides, the lights in the hospital had made my eyes hurt after a while, or maybe that was from all the crying.

Having Ronny home with me meant that the doctors had agreed to discharge her, which meant that she was going to be okay. If they had had any further worries about her, they would have kept her there under observation. She may have broken her arm, but she was going to be all right.

On the other hand, having her home from the hospital had made me hyper aware of all the dangers she faced on a daily basis. I had never been the kind of mom who kept the place 100 percent baby-proofed as their kid grew up, and when we moved into our place in Nebraska, I hadn't been too careful about things figuring that Ronny was old enough to be careful not to slip on the kitchen floor and things like that.

Now, I wanted to go through and pad everything, lock each cabinet and drawer, put down non-slip mats, the whole nine yards. I was terrified she was going to injure herself again, and worse next time. What if it had been her head instead of her arm?

I knew that was no way to raise a child, however. I didn't want Ronny to grow up scared for her life of everything. Still, it was hard to pull back when my mothering instincts were screaming at me to protect her from the world at large.

As much as I hated to admit it, Wes was another thing I wanted to protect her from. She had already asked me about him a couple of times since she'd met him in the hospital. Was she already bonding with him, even though she didn't know that he was her father? If so, what would come of it?

I knew that Wes thought that he wanted to get to know her. What I wasn't sure he understood, though, was that parenting was a full-time thing. You couldn't just be a father when it was convenient.

I wondered if he realized how hard it was to balance parenthood with a career. How many sleepless nights I'd had over the years where I stayed up working on a costume or a school project or something else for Ronny, only to have to go in to work the next day and act as bright and cheerful and alert as ever.

Not that I wanted to martyr myself. I knew Wes. I knew that he could put in the work. It was what had made him such great competition through college. I just wasn't sure that he realized what he was signing himself up for, and I wasn't sure that this was what he really wanted. He had been perfectly happy in his life before Ronny had come along. Once he got to know her, there would be no backing out.

Because if he got to know her and then decided he didn't want to stick around, Ronny was going to be hurt, and that was something I couldn't abide by.

I was trying not to think too hard about the fact that it wasn't just Ronny I was trying to protect. If he left Ronny, if he didn't want to be a part of her life, then he wouldn't be a part of my life either. It was the same thing I'd been trying to protect myself against years ago: that fear of rejection. It was one of the reasons why I hadn't told him about Ronny.

It wasn't fair to him. Especially not since he seemed to actually want this. At the same time, though, I was afraid to trust him, to open up to him. Meanwhile, I was the one who probably shouldn't be trusted, since after all, I had lied to him for a very long time. It was all so confusing.

With Ronny home from the hospital, I knew that meant I had to get back to work. She would be fine at school; I knew that the teachers would look out for her, and she had never had anything bad happen to her there before. Besides, it would be selfish to try to keep her home for a few extra days just to look out for her. She needed to go back to school; she was already going to be far enough behind. Thank God it was still early enough in the year that she would be able to make up for what she had missed.

In any case, Ronny was a ball of energy now that she was no longer cooped up at the hospital. I didn't want to say that she drove me crazy that first day we were back at the house, but I definitely deserved the glass of wine I poured for myself that night.

It would be good for her to be back in school, even if it was hard watching her catch the bus the next morning. With her back in school, though, I had to face Wes again.

I had been thinking over that conversation we'd had at the coffee shop, almost nonstop. I was glad we had gotten some of those things out in the open, but at the same time, I still felt unsure about everything. I knew that work wasn't the place to have a subsequent conversation about it, but I also wasn't sure I could get through a normal workday without at least mentioning some of the things that were on my mind.

Fortunately, everyone still assumed that Wes and I were working on the product line we'd just had the investment pitch for. It was hard to believe that that had only happened earlier this week.

I shut the door carefully behind me as I went to Wes's office, ignoring the daggers that Beth glared at me as I did so. There was a part of me that was curious about that. Had Wes had a prior work relationship? Was that the reason he'd been so quick to say that this had to stay strictly professional between us and that what had happened was a mistake?

I couldn't see Beth as being his type, though. No, she probably just wanted him and couldn't have him. *Too bad for you*, I thought, even though I knew it was childish. The thing was, I still wanted Wes. I was nervous and unsure, but I knew he was a great guy and that I would be lucky to have him. Things were just complicated.

"How's Ronny?" Wes asked immediately when I came in. "Where's Ronny? You didn't have to leave her and come back to work so quickly, you know. I would have given you the rest of the week off."

I couldn't help but smile at him. Something told me he had been almost as worried as I had been over the past couple days. That made me feel a little better about letting him into our lives. Still, there was definitely a conversation there to be had.

"She's at school," I explained. "She was ready to go back." I rolled my eyes and added dryly, "More than ready, in fact. She can't wait to show off her cast to everyone."

Wes laughed. "I guess I probably missed my chance to draw something on there, then?" he joked.

I paused and then cleared my throat. "No, uh. She actually drew a square on there and said she was saving that spot for you." It made my heart jump into my throat to hear her say that. God, I was so worried that he was going to hurt her.

"You don't sound too happy about that," Wes said carefully, accurately guessing at my emotions. How did he know me so well?

I sighed. "Look, you're a great guy, but I just need to make sure you understand all of this," I said, dropping into a seat across from him and pressing my fingertips against my eyelids. For the thousandth time that week, I felt exhaustion creep over me. "Ronny's never had a father before, so she didn't know what she was missing. If something happens now, though, if you decide that you don't want to be part of her life, she's going to be devastated."

Wes narrowed his eyes at me. "What makes you think I'm going to decide I don't want to be part of her life?" he asked, and I could hear the anger barely concealed there in his tone. I was glad he wasn't yelling at me, but at the same time, I felt just as small as he continued. "Have you forgotten that you were the one who left after college? That you're the one who didn't even say goodbye? I'm not you, Rian. It's not fair for you to act like I'm going to disappear when you're the one who keeps doing that."

I swallowed hard, knowing he had a point. Still: "She's already getting attached to you," I said quietly. "I know it's not fair to you, but I can't help but want to protect her, at least until you know what you're getting yourself in for. Can we just not tell her that you're her father, at least for now? Just let her get to know you as a friend first, and then later we can tell her."

Wes scowled at me, and for a moment, I thought he was going to tell me no way. But finally, he shook his head. "Fine," he said, his tone a bit frosty but otherwise civil. "I don't like it, but fine, if that's what you need. I do want to get to know her, though. I want to spend time with her. If you don't let me, I'm sorry, but I will have to get lawyers involved in this."

My head snapped up, and I stared at him, mouth agape. I

had never even considered that he might get lawyers involved. It felt so distrusting of him. Then again, what reason did he have to trust me? I had given him no reason to.

I nodded slowly. "That's... fair," I said. Fairer than I wanted to admit. "I did say you could come over for dinner. Why don't you come over tonight?"

Wes nodded. "That sounds like a good plan," he said. "Now, shall we get to work? There's a few things we need to go over. Devin and the board have a couple changes they'd like to make to the product line."

It was surprisingly easy to put aside all the personal drama and focus on work with Wes. Maybe it was the fact that we had finally cleared the air a little. Still, as we continued to work together, I could feel myself noticing more and more about how attractive he still was. By the time I headed home at the end of the day, I was turned on and tired, and somehow I had to pull it together for dinner that night.

When he arrived, things were still a mess. Ronny was running all over the place like a demon, still excited to be out of the hospital. She was equally excited because all her friends had signed her cast and her teacher had given her chocolate as a get-well present. The house was a mess, and dinner wasn't ready yet. Ronny was bouncing around the kitchen singing at the top of her lungs, so loudly that I didn't even hear the doorbell ring and didn't turn around when she shrieked in excitement.

She launched herself at Wes, who managed to catch her and somehow not jostle her flailing cast in the process.

He twirled her around and then set her carefully back down, giving her an exaggerated bow that had her in stitches. "Hey, you," Wes said, smiling warmly at her. "Looks like you're feeling a little better than the last time I saw you?"

"Uh-huh!" Ronny said proudly. She thrust her cast toward

him. "Look, I saved you a spot. Can you draw a picture now please?"

"That depends. Did your mom already draw hers?" he asked.

"Yup, she drew this kitty cat over here," Ronny explained. "It's because we had a kitty cat when we were in New York, but she couldn't come live with us here because the plane ride was too long, so we left her with Mommy's friends."

"Oh did you?" Wes said. "Well, I think I can draw something better than a kitty cat. How about a unicorn?"

"Yes!" Ronny said. She spun around and ran over to me, tugging on my dress. "Mommy, did you hear that, he's going to draw a unicorn!"

I laughed. "I'll believe it when I see it," I said, even though I knew that Wes was talented at sketching.

Back in college, our little competition had been heated, and I hadn't always appreciated it. But now, there was something cute about him wanting to outdo me in drawing on our daughter's cast. I was smiling as I turned back to the stove.

"Sorry, dinner will be ready soonish," I apologized to Wes. "I've had my hands full."

Wes chuckled. "Don't worry about it," he said. "If all else fails, remember I said that we could order something."

"Like pizza?" Ronny asked, and Wes winced, realizing the mistake he'd made.

"Maybe another night," he said. "I bet what your mom is making is better than pizza, isn't it?"

Ronny cocked her head to the side. "Probably," she agreed. "She's making special food because of you, that's what she told me. Can you draw on my cast now?"

Wes grinned at me, and I was sure he could see my blush. Okay, so I might have mentioned to Ronny that what I was cooking was important because Wes was coming over, but what I meant was that I didn't want to poison the first dinner guest I'd had in ages. That was all.

I knew that explaining that now was only going to make me sound defensive, though, so I let it slide. Besides, the two of them were happily chatting about the unicorn that Wes was going to draw, and I didn't want to interrupt that. They looked so comfortable with one another. *Like family.*

I still couldn't help but feel nervous about all of this. I wondered if maybe my fears were unfounded, though. Maybe Wes was exactly what Ronny needed in her life. After all, he certainly seemed to be just what I needed in my life…

CHAPTER 21

WES

I couldn't believe how well things were going at Rian's place for dinner. I had to admit I had been nervous going into it. I didn't know if things were going to go well with Ronny. After all, she might be my daughter, but I had never really been close to kids before. I didn't know the first thing about how to act around them. Just because we were related, it didn't give me any sort of advantage on that front.

Things were going well, though. It felt totally domestic but surprisingly comfortable at the same time. Like I belonged here, in this place. At this table, with these two remarkable people. We felt like a family. Suddenly, I realized just how much I wanted this. I was sick of coming home alone every evening. I wanted to come home to something like this.

The longer I sat there, though, the more I started to realize just what I had missed out on over the past seven years. For all this time, Rian had *had* this. She had gotten to come home to her daughter and listen to her babble about her favorite television show and what she'd done in school that day. I was the only one who had missed that.

Sure, maybe we could make up for lost time now, but there were some moments I was never going to be able to get back. Rian's pregnancy moments, taking care of her and making sure she was as comfortable as possible. The excitement and anticipation of welcoming a child into the world.

Then everything after that, Ronny's younger years. I had missed her first smile, her first word, her first steps. I had missed her birthdays. I had missed her first day of kindergarten. She was seven years old, and she barely knew me. She would never need me the way that she had needed Rian. I would never be quite as much her parent as Rian was.

She had kept that from me. It was tough to realize that nothing I could do would make up for it now. I would never tell Ronny that Rian had kept me from knowing about her, but at the same time, I didn't want her to think I had chosen not to be there.

I would have been there. It was hard not to resent Rian for her decision to keep quiet about the baby.

On the other hand, I was proud of Rian. She had clearly done a great job raising Ronny, and I knew that as a single parent, it couldn't have been easy. Especially not balancing her career and moving up through the ranks the way she had. It was definitely impressive.

But I could have been there for her. I could have supported her. I could have taken Ronny to her after-school programs or helped around the house, the same way I had tonight when Ronny was bouncing all over the kitchen distracting Rian from finishing up with the dinner preparations. I could have been there. I should have been there.

I wanted to talk to Rian about it, but I also knew I was going to have to tread lightly. I didn't want her to think I was criticizing her for her actions. What was done was done. Still, I wanted her to know that I was here for the long run now. That I wanted to be part of her and Ronny's lives, whatever it took.

I wanted her to know that now that I knew about Ronny, I wasn't going to lose her from my life ever again. I just hoped that Rian would be all right with that and that I wouldn't have to bring her to court on it. I had mentioned that thing about the lawyers without really intending to make it a threat, but if that was what it took, then that was what I was going to have to do.

For now, I tried to focus on tonight. At the same time, I felt like I kept getting flashes of what this might be like if we could keep things going. What a family we could be.

We finished up dinner, and I couldn't help but laugh at the mess that Ronny had made of herself. There was food smeared on her fingers and her cheeks. In fact, it looked like she hadn't so much eaten her dinner as rubbed it all over every available surface.

Rian rolled her eyes fondly at the girl. "One of these days," she sighed.

Ronny looked down at her hands and shirt and shrugged. "Oops," she said, giving a devilish little smile. "It's hard to eat with just one hand."

I snorted, and Rian rolled her eyes, but she definitely looked amused. She lifted Ronny out of her chair, seemingly heedless of the mess but careful of the cast. "Time for a bath, little piglet," she said.

Ronny groaned. "It's not even bedtime yet," she complained. "I wanted to show Mr. Wes all of my get-well cards from school."

"Next time," Rian promised her, and I liked the idea that she might want me to come back again another time. "It's going to take extra time for your bath tonight because we'll have to be careful not to get your cast wet."

Ronny frowned but finally nodded. "Fine," she said, sounding very put-upon.

Rian turned toward me, our daughter balanced on her hip, and my breath caught. I didn't know if I had ever seen anything so beautiful in my life. She looked like the perfect mother, and something about the fact that she was holding my *child* made something tug inside my chest.

"It's going to take a while," she repeated. "You can go if you want. I'll see you at work tomorrow."

I stared at her face, trying to gauge how much she really wanted me out of there. Of course, I wouldn't go so far as to intrude on bath time. I knew we weren't there yet. At the same time, I kept thinking about how tough it must have been to be a single parent for all these years. The least I could do would be to lighten the load a little now, if I could.

I stood up. "Why don't I help with the cleanup instead?" I suggested.

Rian's face registered first surprise and then doubt. "You don't have to," she said. "I can handle it."

"I know you can," I said honestly. Because I was certain she could handle just about anything at this point. She shouldn't have to, though. She had cooked dinner for us, and now she was going to go bathe our daughter and put her to sleep. She shouldn't have to do it all on her own; that wasn't the way a partnership worked.

"I'll clean up," I told her, a bit more firmly this time.

A grateful smile spread across Rian's face. "Thank you," she said. She turned and carried Ronny upstairs. I started cleaning the kitchen as I heard the tub come on and start to fill up. I hummed to myself as I scrubbed the pots, pans, and countertops. I was just wiping down the last plate when Rian poked her head back into the kitchen.

"Ronny's in bed," she said. "She wanted to know if you would read her a story, though."

I smiled. "That would be nice," I said. Again, a warmth suffused my body. For this one precious night, at least, it felt like we were a family. I just hoped that this could last.

I followed Rian upstairs to Ronny's bedroom. "What story did you want me to read?" I asked Ronny.

"*The Giggling Giraffe!*" Ronny answered immediately. "It's my favorite."

Rian snorted. "For this week," she teased.

"Nuh-huh," Ronny said, her eyes wide and serious. "*Forever*. It's my favorite favoritest."

I chuckled and sat down on the edge of her bed. Rian sat next to me, her thigh pressed against mine. I tried not to focus on that sensation and instead looked down at the book that Ronny pressed into my hands. She settled back in bed, snuggling in with the covers pulled up to her chin.

I did my best reading of the story that I could, giving the characters funny voices that made Ronny laugh. She was nearly asleep by the time I finished the book for the second time. I couldn't stop myself from reaching out and brushing back her soft hair. She smiled sleepily at me.

"Good night, kiddo," I murmured.

She hummed an acknowledgment, her eyes sliding shut. For a moment, I watched her, marveling at how perfect she was. I couldn't help feeling a bit emotional as I turned to see Rian watching me carefully. I hoped she could see in my eyes how grateful I was to her for letting me have this experience. I wouldn't trade it for the world.

CHAPTER 22

RIAN

Seeing Wes reading to Ronny melted my heart. She was eating it up, giggling almost constantly the first time through the story. She liked it so much that she asked him to read it again, even. I had to admit, even I was enjoying myself. I knew the story backwards and forwards by this point—Ronny's favorites might change nearly every day, let alone every week, but she had certain ones that she did go back to frequently and *The Giggling Giraffe* story was one of them.

Still, even though I knew the story maybe a bit too well, he gave it new life, and I had to admit I enjoyed it.

It made me think of all the things that could have been different if I had just told him about our daughter. All the things that Ronny had missed out on, and all the things that Wes had missed out on too. I felt guilty.

At the time, I had just assumed that he probably didn't want to be a father. There might even have been a small part of me that tried to pretend he wouldn't be a good one. It was clear now, though, that I had been wrong. If he hadn't wanted to be a father, he wouldn't be anywhere near this good with Ronny. He was doing a phenomenal job with her, and even though it was only one evening, I could tell that he was going to be a good influence on her life.

I should have given him the opportunity to prove all of that earlier.

I couldn't help but feel sad. For the first time, I had to confront the fact that maybe I hadn't made the right choice. Maybe in trying to keep Ronny safe, to keep her from being rejected by a father who might not want her, I had instead hurt her by keeping her away from him. I had denied her her daddy's love.

As he finished up reading the story for the second time and reached forward to brush Ronny's hair back, murmuring a good-night to her, I looked down at my hands, feeling tears prick my eyeballs. I was overcome with the sweetness of his gestures toward her. I was overcome with emotion in general.

For a long time, I had dreamed about what it would be like to someday have a "complete" family, something that was more than just Ronny and me.

Not that she wasn't enough for me, but I had long thought about what it might be like to have a partner to help me out. Sometimes at the end of a long day of work, I didn't want to be the only one looking out for her, and cooking, and cleaning up the house. I just couldn't stay on top of it all, as much as I tried to.

Over the years, I had found a certain balance that normally worked for me, but at the same time... Well, I wasn't about to deny how grateful I was that Wes had cleaned up the kitchen while I gave Ronny her bath. Nor could I deny how nice it had been to sit back and just listen while Wes read Ronny's bedtime story. I felt relaxed and content in a way that I hardly remembered ever feeling.

With all that guilt running through me, though, I had to

face the fact that I didn't deserve Wes. He was way too good for me. He had overlooked that I had lied to him for all those years, and he had really stepped up to the plate. I had invited him over for dinner, and I certainly hadn't asked him to stick around after dinner to help clean up or anything else.

What's more, when he turned to look at me, I could tell how much he appreciated that I had asked him to read to Ronny that night. It meant everything to me to know how much he clearly wanted to be a part of her life.

No, I didn't deserve someone so kind, so understanding. I didn't understand someone who was simultaneously such a great businessman as well as an all-around great guy.

As sure as I was that I didn't deserve him, however, I also knew that I wanted him. Badly. This evening had me thinking about what things might be like if he and I could put aside our differences and build a family. I wasn't sure how things would work with the business side of things. He was still my boss, but surely the fact that we had history that predated my coming to work for him would help our situation?

We'd have to see. For now, all I knew was that I wanted him.

When it became clear that Ronny was fast asleep, we tiptoed out of her room. I grinned over at Wes, and he grinned right back at me. We went down to the kitchen and stood there for a moment. "Can I get you a glass of wine or something?" I asked Wes belatedly.

"Sure," Wes said, shrugging easily. "Or if you want me to get out of your hair, just let me know."

I shook my head. "Stay," I said quietly. I could feel the tension between us, thickening the air. There were some things that we needed to get out before he left. Otherwise, work tomorrow was going to be uncomfortable, both of us wary of the words that hadn't been said. No, we needed to talk. And to be honest, I needed a glass of wine to calm my nerves before that point. I had to admit, I was worried about what might be said.

This was the first night I had let him into the family. This was the make-or-break night for us. What if he decided that he didn't want anything to do with us from here on? The thought made my blood run cold. That possible rejection was even more worrying now that I had seen him with Ronny. Now that I had gotten it in my head what a great dad he would make for her.

I headed into the kitchen and grabbed a bottle of wine, bringing it back out into the living room with a couple of glasses. I sat nervously on the edge of the couch. Wes reached over and lightly laid a hand on my thigh before I could pour the wine.

"I want to be a part of Ronny's life," he said, before the tension could get to be too much. He paused. "Listen, I don't want to pressure you. I know that things are going to take time, and I'm sure that you're still not ready to tell Ronny about the fact that I'm her father. I'm okay with that. I don't love it, but I'm okay with it. That said, I want to be here for her. Eventually, I'd like to be her dad. For right now, though, I'd settle for being part of her life as your friend."

I stared at him for a moment, trying to think of what to say to that. I think I'd been so sure that he was going to tell me that he had reconsidered, that he didn't want any part in this, that my mind took an extra minute to process the fact that he did want to still be part of our lives.

What did that say about me, that I expected that from him?

I didn't mention that now, though. Instead, I nodded slowly. "I would like that," I said softly. "You're right, I'm not quite there with telling Ronny you're her dad. I know she's going to have a lot of questions that I'm not sure how to answer right now. Tonight was good, though."

"I'd like to have more nights like tonight," Wes said.

I nodded. "Me too," I admitted. I smiled at him, feeling almost shy. I tried to think of a way to tell him how much I appreciated all of this. I appreciated the fact that he wanted to be there for Ronny. I appreciated the fact that he wanted to be there for me, and that he had done the cleaning up without me even having to ask him. Most of all, though, I appreciated that he wasn't demanding anything. He was simply asking, allowing me to make the decisions that worked best for us.

Before I could stop myself, I was leaning in to kiss him, the wine and my earlier worries all but forgotten. Things weren't perfect between us just yet, but I had a feeling that things might possibly work out, and that was more than I had ever had before. It was a heady feeling to think that I might actually be able to put together a family with him.

It was a feeling that made my earlier passion for him burn even hotter in my belly.

I knew that we should probably cool things down for a while. Figure out how we could coexist as parents before we added this other level to things. I was afraid that if we rushed into this, things would fizzle out too soon. Where would that leave his relationship with Ronny? I didn't want to mess things up for them by making things awkward between Wes and me.

At the end of the day, though, there was no stopping this. There never had been. There was a reason we had slept together back in college, that night Ronny had been conceived. Somehow, we had gone from archrivals to lovers, and there was no tempering the heat of this desire.

I soon forgot all the reasons why I might want to take things a little slower with him. All it took was the twist of

Wes's tongue against mine, his hand creeping along my hip just along the edge of my panties, the feeling of his strong and solid chest between my splayed fingertips.

I gasped and arched into him. I pushed him back against the arm of the couch and climbed into his lap, straddling him. I could feel how hard he already was, his prick pressed up against my pretty pink panties. I shivered, aching with longing. My mind kept flashing back to those warm feelings of contentedness I had been feeling all evening, watching him with Ronny, imagining a future with him.

I wanted him. Body, soul, everything. There was no denying it.

Wes slid his hand along my ass, cupping my cheeks, spreading me slightly. I could feel the cool breeze against my damp entrance, and I moaned softly, biting my lower lip to contain the sound.

Wes chuckled softly, giving a meaningful look toward the stairs. "Maybe we should go upstairs," he suggested in a husky voice. "Might be some awkward questions to answer if Ronny hears us and comes down to this."

I giggled breathlessly, feeling only vaguely ashamed even though I could just picture what a mess we would make of things if Ronny did walk in on us right now. What a way to broach the subject that he was her dad...

I gave Wes one final kiss and then rolled off of him, holding out a hand to him. I paused, holding his hand, waiting for the apprehension to come back. Maybe we were taking things too quickly. Maybe we ought to hold off on this for now.

The worries didn't return, though. Instead, I merely felt excited. I wanted to know what, exactly, this might lead to. More than anything.

I tugged at his hand, grinning as I all but dragged him toward the stairs. Wes chuckled softly as he followed.

CHAPTER 23

WES

I t was a wonder that we managed to make it to Rian's room before succumbing to the pleasure racing through us. I could tell she was just as hot as I was, just as primed and ready to go. Something about this evening seemed to have woken something in both of us. Maybe it was some primordial sense of oneness, the feeling that we were actually a family and that we belonged together. Maybe it was just the realization that we really could bring out the best in one another.

Whatever it was, making out on the couch had been steamier than I could possibly have imagined, and by the time Rian grabbed my hand to lead me upstairs, I could feel every pulse of electricity. I couldn't stop myself from grabbing her and kissing her as we made our way upstairs. I would have stripped her naked and had her right there in the hall if it hadn't been for Ronny sweetly sleeping somewhere in the house.

I was breathless and hard by the time we tumbled into bed together. I nearly tore Rian's clothes ripping them off her prone form. There was no patience left in either of our movements. There just couldn't be. We were too close to the edge already.

I forced myself to slow things down, kissing my way across her skin. I still had that terrifying feeling that this meant more than anything that had come before. If I messed this up now, who knew if I would ever get it again. I had no wish for this to be the last time, but on the other hand, if it did end up being that way, then I wanted her to know, at the very least, how much I appreciated tonight.

She didn't have to let me in so easily. She didn't have to let me come over for dinner and bond with her daughter in front of her. But she had opened her life to me. There was something to be said for that.

I wanted her to know how much I wanted more, too. I wanted her to realize how good we could be for one another. I wanted her to know what a future with me could be like, even if tonight was only a glimpse of it.

I stared into her eyes as I fingered her slick core, watching each little change to her expression, listening to each quiet sound that fell from her lips, edging her ever closer to explosive pleasure. I didn't think I had ever seen anything more beautiful than the way she looked spread out across those dove-gray sheets, arching her back, her creamy skin in sharp relief against the darkness of the night, lit only by moonlight.

I knew she was close, but I was surprised when her body tensed, her mouth falling open on a soft gasp. Her head fell to the side, and she rubbed a hand against her face, overcome by pleasure. I could feel her walls twitching around my thrusting digits as she rocked crazily onto my hand, cumming hard, her folds gushing with even more wetness than before.

I growled, unable to hold myself back for another moment. My cock needed no additional stroking to get it to full hardness. I pushed into her while her walls were still quaking with their earlier relief. She groaned out a breathy *yesss* and wrapped her legs around me, pulling me even closer to her, drawing me farther inside of her warmth.

I had no more patience for finesse; I needed this. I set a rapid rhythm, knowing full well that I wouldn't last. Then again, she had already cum once—or was it twice now? I would be well within my rights to chase my own orgasm now.

And that was just what I did. I moved like I had never moved before, rocking into her in quick, sharp, shallow thrusts. I pressed a hand over her mouth as her cries spiraled louder and louder. I was vaguely aware of the fact that our daughter was there somewhere in the house. Our daughter. Because Rian and I were linked and always would be.

It was the thought of that deeper connection that sent me over the edge. I spilled for what felt like forever, waves of ecstasy that were nearly more than I could handle. I fell panting to the sheets, sweaty with exertion. Rian flung out an arm, finding me in the darkness, curling toward me. I pulled her into my arms, stroking her hair with my damp fingers.

Falling asleep with Rian in my arms was the capper on top of an already perfect evening. There had been sweetness, there had been sexiness. Overall, it was everything I wanted, for the rest of my life. If only I could find some way to make this last.

The last thought I had before I drifted off to sleep was that I was pretty sure things were going to be all right. We might not have worked out all the details just yet, but I had a feeling that things weren't out of our reach. I had a feeling we could find some way to make things work.

And I sure hoped that would prove to be true. I didn't know what I would do otherwise; I already couldn't picture my life without these two perfect angels in it.

The following morning, I smiled to wake up with Rian in my arms. I nuzzled her cheek, lightly kissing her forehead. But then, I looked past her and saw the time on the clock. I swore and scrambled backward, untangling myself from her.

"What's wrong?" Rian asked, looking sleepily toward the clock. Her eyes widened. "You have a meeting," she said, as though I might not have realized. She started babbling apologies. "I forgot to set an alarm, I'm so sorry. I should have known better."

"Don't worry about it," I said, giving her a quick kiss as I fumbled the buttons on my shirt closed. I was really glad we didn't seem to have done any damage to it the night before or this could be really awkward. "Neither of us was thinking about it." It was no more Rian's fault than mine.

In fact, it was more my fault than hers. She might have been the one who started the make-out session downstairs, but I was an adult and I had known what my schedule looked like for this morning. I should have been thinking about it.

The truth was, I hadn't woken up this late in years now. I hadn't slept that well, or that deeply, in years now either. Something about Rian...

I pushed those thoughts away for now. The last thing I needed was to get distracted and end up back in bed with her. I didn't have time for that right now. I was already going to be cutting it close if I wanted to make it to my meeting on time.

Rian rolled out of bed as I was finishing dressing, pulling on a silky, navy blue robe. She stood on her tiptoes and kissed me on the cheek. "All right if I come into work a little late today, boss?" she asked teasingly.

I snorted and kissed her properly on the lips, allowing myself to linger there for maybe a second longer than was wise. When it came to Rian, though, it seemed like all my logic went out the window. "See you later," I told her.

Fortunately, I made it to my meeting with two minutes to spare. I should have known that wearing yesterday's clothes wouldn't go unnoticed, however. They weren't the same clothes I'd worn to work the previous day; I'd gone home and changed before dinner. But my shirt was wrinkled from spending the night in a heap on the floor, and from head to toe, I knew that I probably looked a little unkempt and haphazard.

Sure enough, Beth called me out on it as soon as I came out of the meeting, raising an eyebrow at me. "You look... casual today," she said, her voice dripping with barely veiled meaning.

I fought the urge to roll my eyes. "Couldn't find my iron," I lied, my tone just as dry. With a hard look, I challenged her to say something else about it.

To my surprise, she did: "Guess you didn't make it home from Rian's last night? What did you do, sleep on the couch in your clothes?" she asked.

I blinked at her. "How did you know I was at Rian's?" I asked, glad that she had at least kept her tone down somewhat while accusing me of something that could probably get me fired.

"You were there for dinner, according to your calendar," Beth said.

I nearly swore out loud. I had forgotten that she had access to that calendar or I never would have been that specific about my plans for the evening. It wasn't like I had needed any reminder of it anyway; I had mainly put it in there so that Beth wouldn't try to schedule me for a work dinner with some of our clients.

I had been stupid, in retrospect. And Beth might have accused me of having slept on the couch in my clothes, but from the way her eyes had narrowed with jealousy, it was clear she had another suspicion about what the sleeping arrangements had looked like.

"What I do outside of work is none of your business," I said, trying to make my tone as firm as I could. I couldn't let her know that I felt guilty knowing that my carelessness could have gotten both me and Rian in a lot of trouble with the company. If Beth knew I was guilty, it was only a matter of time before she tried to use the knowledge against me.

Beth's eyes widened in feigned innocence. "I was just trying to make sure you didn't miss any appointments," she said. "I would never do anything like go snooping through your personal business. After all, we're friends as well as coworkers. I like to think so, at least."

I frowned. It was on my lips to tell her that we weren't friends. She was just my employee, and only because I had inherited her from George. I knew that wasn't something she wanted to hear, though, and the last thing I needed was to give her another reason to be jealous or to go to HR about the dinner I'd had with one of my coworkers the night before.

I tried to remember what, exactly, I had put into the appointment I'd made in the calendar. To my relief, I didn't think I had specified the place or mentioned any details of it. Maybe I could play it off as a meeting of coworkers if I had to. Something about it being a planning meeting, or else something about a celebration dinner after the success of our pitch in New York. Hell, maybe I could even get Devin to vouch for me.

Would he do that, if it came down to it? I knew he liked working with me, and liked working with Rian even more. But then again, with me out of the picture, he might think that he would have better access to her. Except that he must realize that if I got into hot water over this, she would, too?

I felt sick at the fact that I even had to think about things like this. I knew I should never have gotten involved with Rian. Things had spun out of control way too quickly. How could I pull back now, though, when I knew the secret she had been keeping for all these years was the fact that we had a daughter together?

Things the night before had gone so well, and it only made me want more with her. Was I ready to risk my career for this, though?

In any case, if I was risking my career, I didn't want Beth to be the first person at work to know about it. So I told her a lie about the reason for the dinner: "It was a planning meeting," I told her. "I didn't put any more specific details on there because what we're working on is still a secret. I don't want anyone to be able to leak anything to one of our competitors."

Even as I said it, the lie sounded weak. After all, that just wasn't the way that I did business. I trusted everyone who worked for me. What's more, I didn't want anyone in the company to believe I didn't trust all of them. That was no way to stoke company morale.

"Please stay out of my private business," I said to Beth one more time before retreating to my office. I couldn't help feeling like she had won this round. And what's more, I couldn't help feeling that I had revealed too much about everything. It was Beth's job to handle my personal calendar so she could make sure there were no scheduling conflicts there. Even if there usually weren't, it would look suspicious for me to revoke her access now, especially if George had always been open with her.

The question was, how much had I revealed, and how much proof would she need to bring things crashing down for me and Rian? Did she have enough motivation to ruin things, or would her sense of self-preservation keep her quiet for now?

I had to hope for the latter, even though I knew she was jealous of Rian, given Beth's own unrequited crush on me. I realized now that I probably should have been sterner with her from the start, even if I had been afraid to rock the boat too much when George had handed the company over to me.

It was too late to change things now, though. Things would happen the way that they were meant to. I just hoped I hadn't cost me and Rian that beautiful future I had imagined just last night. I wanted that future more than I could say.

CHAPTER 24

RIAN

I found myself humming on my way into work that morning. The previous night had been as close to perfect as I ever could have hoped for, and I really had the feeling that things between me and Wes might actually work out the way I wanted them to. Waking up next to him had been nice, even in spite of his hasty exit when he had realized what time it was. I had felt bad for that, but he had made it clear he didn't think it was my fault.

In any case, I couldn't blame him for rushing out; I knew he had to get to work. I did, too, and I needed to get Ronny in to school. She was already late for her first class. It was worth it, though, and the school bought my lie about letting her sleep in to rest up after the hospital.

I made it to work as quickly as I could, and even though I hadn't missed anything important, not being the one with meetings that morning, I couldn't help feeling naughty as I came in. If only they all knew what I had done with my night. If only they knew how I had woken up.

Not that I would ever tell anyone that, not even Angie—or at least not yet. What Wes and I had was private, just between us, and that almost made it all even more special. It was another secret, but this was one I felt better about keeping.

The day went by quickly, and when I got a text from Wes at the end of it telling me that he wanted to spend some time with Ronny over the weekend, it only made me smile even more. I liked the fact that he was already thinking about being there for her as much as he could. There was a part of me that was still a little worried, and I knew it was just my motherly protectiveness kicking in. I didn't want anyone to hurt Ronny, and I had never really had to let anyone else in before.

Then again, I had managed to be okay with the idea that she was going off to school, spending more time with her classmates than she sometimes did with me, and I had managed to leave her alone with Angie while I went to New York to close the deal with Devin. So I supposed I could get used to the idea of this as well, if I gave it enough time.

Besides, I wanted this. I was still fantasizing about a future with Wes, and the more I thought about it, the more I wanted it.

Reality turned out to be even better than my fantasies. The weather turned unseasonably nice over the weekend, and Wes ended up taking me and Ronny to the park for a picnic. I had to laugh at the gesture, when Wes showed up with the picnic basket on Saturday morning. "Sorry," I said, seeing his affronted expression, "I'm just trying to picture any guy in New York taking us for a picnic."

Wes frowned. "Central Park, isn't that a thing? I thought people went on picnics there."

"Maybe," I allowed. "But not when they're newly dating."

The words slipped out easily, and I couldn't regret them when I saw the teasing twinkle they brought to Wes's eyes. "Newly dating, huh?" he asked. "Is that what we're doing?"

I shrugged evasively. "Maybe," I said.

"I guess I'll have to bring flowers next time," he said.

I snorted. "Wes Brown, are you a hidden romantic?" I couldn't help asking. Because really, I needed to know what I was getting myself in for. Guy starts showing up with flowers and things starts to feel a little serious, you know?

Wes grinned crookedly at me. "I don't think there's anything hidden about it," he said, winking at me. Just then, Ronny came running into the hall and flung herself toward Wes, who barely had time to pass me the basket before he scooped her up into his arms. "Hey, you," he said, blowing a raspberry on her cheek that had her shrieking with giggles in no time.

He continued in his role of Super Dad while we were at the park. Ronny laughed, thrilled, as he pushed her on the swings, then shrieked with giggles as he chased her all around like an overprotective hen, clucking comically the whole way.

It was adorable, and my chest ached. Soon, my face ached, too, with the force of my smiles. He stayed over on Saturday night, but we didn't have sex again, just cuddled naked in bed together. Somehow, there was something equally intimate about that.

The next morning, I made breakfast for all of us while he fixed a couple things around the apartment that had been driving me nuts since we moved in. I couldn't help but wonder what it would be like to have this forever. I had never had a partner before. To be honest, when Ronny was born, I had almost given up on the idea of it, sure that it would just be me and her for at least as long as it took for her to grow up.

Suddenly, I wasn't sure that had to be the case. Nor was I sure I had ever *wanted* for it to be the case. I had just been scared. I wasn't so scared anymore. Or at least, I was scared in different ways, ones that didn't seem to matter quite as much.

I was in love with Wes. And what's more, there was a huge part of me that was screaming that I should just trust him. I might not know where things would lead, and I knew of course there were still tons of things that we were going to have to work out. Like the fact that he was my boss, for one. Or whether or not he had actually forgiven me for keeping Ronny a secret for all these years. We were going to have to find some way to tell Ronny that he was her dad, even if that meant admitting I had been hiding something from her for all these years.

Still, at the end of the day, I knew that Wes was worth fighting for, and if there was anything I could do to convince him to take a chance on me, I was going to do it. I didn't have a choice; I was endlessly in love with him.

I didn't want the weekend to end, but as I headed into work on Monday, I found I was still smiling with the promise of what might be in store in the future. We had left things on a good note, and I had a feeling it was only a matter of time before I had Wes over again.

I had to admit, I was a little nervous about the meeting I had that afternoon. It was one of the first meetings I would have with Wes at work since things had really heated up between us. I liked to think we were both of an age and maturity level that we could put our attraction aside for now and focus on the task at hand. Especially since we wouldn't be alone in the meeting and Devin would be joining us.

On the other hand, when had I ever been able to turn off my attraction to Wes? We were both going to have to be careful not to do anything that might betray our personal attachments to the company's latest investor. I didn't want to think about what could happen if Devin realized Wes and I had slept together, or that we were sort-of-dating.

Wes was running late to the meeting, and I couldn't help but feel a little relieved at that. If I could just settle into the work thing before he got there, chat with Devin as though everything was normal, I had a feeling I could hold it together once Wes arrived as well.

"How is your daughter?" Devin asked immediately when he came in. "Wes told me she was in the hospital and that was why you needed to leave? I didn't even realize you had a daughter!"

I laughed nervously. I had expected the question but wasn't really sure how to explain things to him. I couldn't tell him why I had been so set on keeping Ronny a secret, so I had to hope he would buy the excuse I gave: "I try really hard to keep my personal life separate from my professional life. As a female in this field, things can get a little tricky sometimes."

"I'm very sorry if that's an experience you've had in the past," Devin said, looking and sounding sincere. "I can assure you that that isn't the experience you'll have working with our company. I couldn't care less what biological parts you have as long as you get the job done. And in fact, I think your femininity could be an asset. You think in different ways. Especially as a mother. We need that sort of creativity and that access to a broader demographic."

There was a part of me that resented the way he said that. Like the only reason I was good at my job was because I had "access to a broader demographic." I knew he didn't mean it that way, though. And besides, I should be grateful that he seemed to accept my little lie.

So instead of chewing him out, I just said, "Anyway, thank you for asking, but Ronny is doing okay. She broke her arm, but it could have been a lot worse. You can't keep her spirits down, and she's already back in school." I rolled her eyes. "I wouldn't be surprised if one of these days I came home to find out that somehow she got the mayor himself to sign her cast; she's got that much charisma."

Devin chuckled. "She gets it from her mom, I'm sure," he said.

I barely stopped myself from saying, "Or her dad." The last thing I needed was to open that can of worms. For obvious reasons, I wasn't about to tell Devin who her dad was—that he would be joining us in the meeting room soon, hopefully—but at the same time, I didn't want to lie to him any more than I had to.

It was a tricky situation.

"So, we've got quite a bit of work to do," I said, steering the conversation toward the purpose of the meeting.

"When will Wes be joining us anyway?" Devin asked curiously. "Wouldn't want to make any of the important decisions without him."

I grinned and glanced at my phone, but there were no new messages there. "He was out at George's place—the founder of the company. Wes has taken over as CEO lately, but George is still technically in charge. I think they were talking about George's ideas for the product line as well. Basically getting his blessing on everything."

"Fair enough," Devin said. "Well, let's get to work. We can catch him up when he gets here."

"Sure," I said easily. We fell into an easy discussion that soon turned excited, with both of us standing at the boardroom's whiteboard writing out different ideas as we brainstormed and bounced ideas back and forth.

"That's perfect!" Devin said as we hit on a brilliant solution to one of our biggest problems with the line. He reached out for a high five and pulled me into a quick hug. I grinned at him as we pulled apart, but I practically jumped out of my skin as Wes cleared his throat at the doorway.

"Wes!" I said, trying not to sound too surprised. Did he

think that I sounded guilty? Nothing had happened; it was just a quick hug between friends. But it was clear from Wes's expression that he wasn't thrilled by the scene he had walked in on, and I couldn't help but feel bad even though I knew that it wasn't my fault.

I'd talk to him about it later, I resolved. Still, I couldn't help feeling a little frustrated as the rest of the meeting proceeded awkwardly, with Wes acting strange.

Nothing had *happened*. Didn't he trust me? What did he think was going to happen, that I was going to jump Devin right here in the middle of the office, where anyone could walk in on us? When Wes and I had a kid together and were sort-of-dating? I would never do something like that.

He might not have forgiven me for having kept Ronny a secret from him for all of those years, but that didn't give him any right to act like this toward me. Not only that, but the more he acted jealous and possessive, the more likely it was to become obvious to Devin and everyone else that Wes and I had slept together. That our relationship wasn't strictly professional.

I couldn't help but feel frustrated with him for blowing the whole hug thing out of proportion. What the hell.

I had a daughter. I couldn't get caught up in drama like this. I didn't want to lose him because of something stupid like this. If a hug was all it took for him to mistrust me, then maybe this wasn't a good idea.

I could feel myself growing more and more agitated as the meeting wore on. Maybe I should talk to him. But at the end of the day, if he had a problem, it was his problem to deal with. I didn't have to be part of this. So when the meeting ended, I said an easy goodbye to Devin, giving him another quick hug. I told Wes I had a few things I needed to take care of that afternoon but that he knew where to find me if he needed me.

Maybe it was childish of me. Maybe I was just avoiding having to talk about the issue. I kept trying to remind myself it wasn't my issue, but I still felt deflated compared to how I had felt that morning. Maybe this relationship thing wasn't all it was cracked up to be. Maybe I had been right, after all, to keep Ronny a secret. We didn't need jealousy or mistrust in our lives.

Telling myself that didn't make me feel any better, though.

"Whoa, what happened in there?" Angie asked as I headed back to my office.

I shook my head. "Just a lot to think about," I told her tersely. I shut myself in my office without saying more to her, hoping she didn't think that I was upset at *her*. I just didn't know what to say right now, not having told her about the weekend I'd had with Wes.

Maybe it had been wrong to keep that a secret from her. Suddenly, I was so sick of secrets. But what could I do about it, really? I couldn't risk my job, and in any case, there was no point risking it if Wes and I were going nowhere in our relationship. There was no winning either way.

CHAPTER 25

WES

I knew I needed to focus on work during this meeting. Devin was an important client, and the last thing I needed was for him to realize anything was off between me and Rian. At the same time, though, it was hard to put my personal feelings aside in light of the scene I had walked in on.

I wanted to give Rian the benefit of the doubt. No, more than that—I didn't want to feel like I was giving her the benefit of the doubt. I wanted to *know* she didn't feel anything for Devin. That the hug had been innocent, and that she hadn't initiated it. I was sure that even if she did think Devin was attractive, she wouldn't start something with him right there in the workplace, not when she had a kid with me, and not when things were already so stressful and out of line with the whole work thing.

If she and *I* weren't supposed to be doing anything there, then it would be even worse if she had a kid with me and then decided to start something with one of our most important clients.

That said, I couldn't stop myself from wondering if

maybe I was being an idiot. Just because Rian had my baby, it didn't mean that we were destined to have a future together. After all, she hadn't even wanted me to know about Ronny. It was just a coincidence that I had found out about her. Maybe Rian had been hoping, for all these years, to find something more.

I couldn't stop myself from feeling jealous. I didn't like the fact that Devin was touching her, and I didn't like the fact that Rian looked so comfortable there.

I wanted to trust her, that was the thing. But she had kept such a major secret from me, for seven whole years. What if Ronny wasn't the only secret she had been keeping?

The worst part of it all was that I could tell from the looks Rian kept giving me that she knew exactly what was going through my mind. Not only that, but she was pissed about it. What could I say, though? I couldn't help feeling jealous. Besides, it wasn't like we had really worked through our problems yet. I had wanted to do that the other night, when I told her that I wanted to be part of Ronny's life. Instead, we had ended up having sex.

Not that I was complaining about that, but we should probably have cooled the jets a bit and talked things through a little more before we just jumped into things like that. Now, all I could focus on were the unknowns. Maybe Rian didn't really want me in her life long-term. I knew better than to wonder whether Ronny was even mine; she looked too much like me not to be.

At the end of the day, though, that wasn't enough to mean that Rian and I could put together a relationship. There were reasons that she had kept my daughter from me for all of those years, and I was still just starting to understand what those reasons were.

"All right, what's going on?" Devin asked after Rian all but ran out of there.

I looked at him in surprise, even though I knew that my distractions must have been obvious. I shook my head. Devin and I might be on pretty good terms, but this wasn't the kind of thing I could tell him about. Even if I didn't get the feeling that he might be interested in Rian, there would be nothing professional about telling him that I had banged her a few times (and oh yeah, knocked her up with a kid back in college).

Devin rolled his eyes, folding his arms across his chest. "Come on," he said. "When you guys were in New York, you were all excited about this project. What changed? Did you get a better offer? You can tell me, you know. I'd like to think that we're friends in addition to being business colleagues."

I sighed. His words made me feel guilty. We were friends. Heck, he had let me drag him off fishing while he was in Nebraska the first time. Yet here I was getting all jealous and bothered because I had a suspicion that he liked Rian. What was worse was that I had a feeling if he knew the whole story, he would have backed off immediately, regardless of his personal feelings.

At the same time, it wasn't like I could tell him about all of that. I was her boss, and there were some lines that you just weren't supposed to cross. "I recently got some big news that I guess I'm still sort of processing," I finally admitted reluctantly, knowing he wasn't going to give up. He was a good friend, and he just wanted to be there for me.

Fortunately, that vague answer did the trick. Devin clapped me on the shoulder. "You know I'm here for you if you need to talk," he said sympathetically.

I felt even more like a heel, but I managed a wan smile. "Thanks," I said.

We parted ways and I headed back to my office. I was surprised when Beth followed me into my office and shut the door behind her. I raised an eyebrow at her, too tired to think of anything to even ask.

Fortunately, I didn't need to ask anything. Beth was practically overflowing with what she wanted to say. "How was your meeting?" she asked. Without giving me a chance to answer, she continued, "You know, people are really starting to talk about Devin and Rian."

"What about them?" I asked suspiciously.

"You know, their secret relationship," Beth said. "I wouldn't say anything about it to you because I know it's none of my business, but it would be one thing if she was just trying to marry him for his money or something. But some people think that Rian is trying to get a job at Devin's firm." She paused, grinning like the cat that got the cream. "Of course, I know how important she is here, and that we can't really afford to lose her. Where would we find another innovations manager?"

I stared at her, flabbergasted to hear her voicing the same sorts of suspicions that had been running through my head when I had come into the boardroom to find Devin hugging Rian. Was there maybe a glimmer of truth there? But no, I was sure it was just gossip.

In any case, it was none of Beth's business. She might have something to gain from the idea that Rian was interested in Devin, since I had a feeling that Beth wanted me and must realize that I was interested in Rian. At the end of the day, though, I didn't have time for gossip in my workplace, and that was all that this was.

"Don't they seem awfully friendly?" Beth pressed. That gave me the opening I needed.

"Friendliness isn't proof of anything," I said sternly. "Devin and I are friendly as well, but you don't think that I'm looking to quit my job here, do you?"

Beth raised an eyebrow at me and wordlessly produced a

printed-out piece of paper. I stared at it for a moment, wondering what the hell it could be, but it was self-explanatory enough. An email from Rian to Devin, asking about possible openings at his firm.

Maybe there was more proof there than I was letting myself realize.

I felt like I was losing my mind. Here I had been thinking that things were good between me and Rian, and she was just scheming to do whatever she could to move back to New York. To take my daughter away from me again, and to shut me out of her life.

The real question was, how could I have been so naïve? Disappearing in the middle of the night, that was her act. She had done it once, and I knew she would do it again. Hell, she certainly hadn't stuck around after the first time we had sex when she returned to Nebraska.

All my insecurities from before came back to me. There must have been some real reason that she didn't tell me about Ronny. She didn't think I was good enough to be her father, and she didn't want me around to be her partner either. She was after someone like Devin, someone handsome and charming who had a ton of money.

Did she have to go behind my back to get with him, though? Did she really have to start sleeping with me as a backup option while she was scheming to leave me again?

I knew I should say something to Beth, that I should remind her again that this was none of her business or something. Maybe remind her that if Rian did want to leave, that was her prerogative. Maybe I should even let Beth know that I had expected from the very start that Rian would want to leave sooner rather than later, because that was just what she did.

I didn't want to talk to Beth now, though. I had too many emotions coursing through me, and the one that bubbled to the surface the most was betrayal. I stalked past Beth and left my office, heading straight for Rian's.

I shut the door behind me, doing my best not to slam it. "What the hell," I said, and for a moment, that was all I could say, anger getting the better of me.

Rian frowned at me, folding her arms defensively across her chest and giving me a cool look. "I didn't do anything wrong," she said carefully.

"You didn't do anything wrong?" I exploded. "Just led me on, let me pretend like you were letting me into your life, when meanwhile you've been planning to leave this whole time. I guess New York is too much of a draw for you—is that it? God, I'd almost like to believe that that's it."

"What are you even talking about?" Rian asked impatiently.

"I saw the email you wrote to Devin, asking him for a job," I sneered. "Look, I'm not an idiot. I knew from the moment that you showed up in my office that you weren't planning on sticking around. I came this close to firing you right then, but I decided to give you a chance. But seriously, using your position here to scheme your way into another one, and meanwhile sleeping with the boss?"

Rian stared at me in shock. She probably didn't expect to get caught. She thought she could just do what she had done time and time again: just make her own plans without any regard for how they would affect me. From her post-grad internship to Ronny to this new job search, it was one secret on top of another. I was done with it.

"And what, when you start working for Devin, you start sleeping with him, too?" I asked bitterly. "Is that the real reason you lost your job in New York—you were fired for sleeping with the boss?"

I knew the second the words were out of my mouth that I shouldn't have said them. I might as well have told her I didn't think she was worthy of her position, that the only reason she had made it from her internship to a real career was that she had slept with the right people. That wasn't fair. I knew she had talent.

Sure enough, Rian's face turned a ghastly shade of white. "You asshole," she hissed, but I could see the tears forming in her eyes.

My shoulders slumped. Suddenly, all the anger left me. I turned half away from her. "If you want to leave, just do it," I said. "I can't stop you. But maybe next time you'll think about telling me?"

I wanted to ask for more, but I could tell she already had her mind made up. She wanted to go back to New York. I wasn't good enough for her, and I never had been. There was nothing I could do about it.

We would figure out how to make things work between us, even if it meant split custody. That much I knew I had a right to. The rest of it, well. I never should have gone against my misgivings and let her in. This heartache I felt now was my own stupid fault. I was just glad I hadn't ruined my career over this.

Rian was silent, but I couldn't bear to look at her to try to figure out what she was thinking. Instead, I turned to leave.

CHAPTER 26

RIAN

Anger boiled inside me as I watched Wes turn to leave my office. What, he thought he could storm in there with all these accusations and then act like he was the one who was hurt? Where did he get off?

I hadn't done anything with Devin. Period. I hadn't been overly friendly, I hadn't thought for a second about sleeping with him, and I certainly hadn't approached him about a job. Did I sometimes think about going back to New York? Sure. My whole life had been there for years, and there were things I missed about it.

At the end of the day, though, there was a reason I had come back to Nebraska. I knew this was where I wanted to raise Ronny, and she was loving it here. I had no plans to leave. In fact, I was picturing a future here with Wes. A future where we lived together in a cute little home here in Nebraska, raising our daughter.

In my mind, I hadn't quite figured out the whole work situation because I knew there was plenty we needed to talk about. Maybe long-term, it would be better for me to work for someone else. Wes and I couldn't keep things a secret forever.

I hadn't started looking for other jobs, though. I especially hadn't started looking for jobs with Devin. Nor was I looking to sleep with him or anyone else other than Wes. This jealousy thing had gone too far.

"Look, I thought we were both adults," I spat. "I shouldn't have to defend myself against these ridiculous accusations that I'm trying to sleep with someone else. Jealousy doesn't look good on you. I'm also not looking to work for anyone else, although now, I don't know, maybe I should be."

"Oh bullshit," Wes said, rolling his eyes. "Not looking for other jobs? I've got proof!" His eyes narrowed. "How many other things have you been lying about?" he asked. "How you got the internship? You kept Ronny a secret from me—how many other things are you hiding?"

I stared at him, suddenly feeling defeated. I realized then, in that moment, that he would never trust me again. Keeping Ronny a secret had permanently damaged the trust between us, and without trust, there was nothing to build a relationship on.

I felt tears prick my eyes. My chest constricted, and I tried to remember if there was a time I had ever felt this sad before. I knew there wasn't, though. I had never felt a heartache like this before, had never lost someone who meant so much to me before. I was absolutely crushed to think that it might be over with him before it ever really started.

And to think that the weekend had gone so well. Who had I been trying to kid, though, acting like we could have something permanent? I really, truly messed things up.

It wasn't just the relationship either. I stared down at the floor. "If you can't trust me, then there's no point in me staying in this position," I said flatly. It was the truth, as much as I hated to admit it. I wanted this job, but there was no way that he and I were going to be able to work together professionally after all of this. I couldn't handle seeing him every day, tantalizingly close but further away than ever before.

Logically, the innovations manager couldn't be at odds with the CEO. That just wasn't how good businesses worked. We needed to be able to collaborate, and right now, that seemed impossible.

"I'm resigning," I said softly, the words bitter on my tongue. "Effective immediately."

I felt numb as I left the office, Wes staring after me. I kept my head down as I went to my car. I didn't know what was coming next. Contrary to what Wes seemed to believe, I hadn't been looking for other positions. I supposed maybe I could call up some of the other companies that had been interested in hiring me before, but I didn't like the thought of uprooting Ronny.

Maybe this was the end of my career, as well as the end of my relationship. Clearly it wasn't working out for me anyway. Perhaps it was time for a change.

Wes caught up to me in the parking lot. "What the hell are you doing?" he snapped, blocking me as I tried to get to my car. "Or rather, I'm the one being childish? You can't just walk out of a job with no notice, whatever your relationship with the boss might be. What are you going to do about Ronny? Unless you've already secured the job with Devin, so you don't need this one?"

I stared at him. "For the last time, there is no job with Devin," I said. But there was no anger left in me, just dull acceptance that this was the way things were going to end. "I made a mistake in not telling you about Ronny," I continued. "I wasn't trying to run out on this, though." I shrugged broadly. "I guess this was just a mistake—isn't that what you said?"

I stepped around him and opened the door to my car, desperate to get away from him before I started crying. I knew I didn't have much longer. It felt like the whole world was crashing down around me. I didn't even know where to begin to put things back together.

"I will take you to court, if I have to," Wes threatened as I slipped into my seat. He held the door open, keeping me from leaving. "I meant it when I said that I want to be part of Ronny's life. Whatever I have to do to make sure I get that, I'm going to do it. You can't just run away from this like you did in college."

I scowled at him and gave the door a hard yank. He quickly pulled his fingers out of the way. I didn't look back to see his expression. I didn't want to know.

I wanted to get out of there. I wanted to pretend like this had never happened, like it was all a bad dream. How had things gone so wrong so quickly? I felt sick as I thought back to how great things had been. I knew that Ronny would ask me when she would get to see Wes again. What would I say to her?

What was I going to do?

I started driving, not paying any attention to where I was going. It wasn't long before I had to pull over as the tears started, sobs wrenched from my body. I already missed him. It had been hard enough to get over him after that one night in college.

What the hell was I going to do? I had no idea.

CHAPTER 27

WES

I felt like shit. There was no denying it. The fact that there was nothing I could do to fix things only made it all the worse.

In my head, I kept picturing Rian driving away. At least I had gotten to watch her leave this time. There was no question about whether she might come back. No, she was gone for good. The next time I saw her, it would likely be during a custody battle.

God, that was the last thing I wanted to get tangled up in. Even more so because I knew as soon as I went to the lawyers and tried to fight her for a chance to see my daughter, the secret would be out. Everyone would know that Rian and I had a daughter. My business life would never be the same again.

I hadn't been the one to hire Rian, but I hadn't said anything to HR when she came on. I hadn't even said anything to them after I found out about Ronny. I hadn't been sure what to say yet. Now, though, I was sure it would look like some sort of gross omission.

Not only that, but it was bound to come out at some

point that she and I had been sleeping together while she was working for me. If the custody battle turned ugly, maybe she would use it as proof that I wasn't a good role model to be around our daughter or something like that.

It made me sick to think about. I hated the thought that I might lose her and my job. Well, really, losing my job was a minimal pain to the thought of losing her again. There was nothing that I could do about it, though. I could never trust her, which meant that even if I hadn't been an absolute ass to her, a meaningful relationship between the two of us would just never be possible.

If it had just been jealousy, that would have been one thing. We could probably have handled that. But finding out she was looking for jobs elsewhere, that she was already planning on leaving again, that she'd had one foot out the door this whole time? That was inexcusable. I still didn't like that she had left after college, but that I could forgive her for. She'd had an opportunity that she couldn't turn down, one that I would never have asked her to turn down.

We were too old to keep living like that, though. And there was a difference between leaving because she had already found a position in a company and actively searching for a different pace of work while she was sleeping with me.

The worst thing was that at the end of the day, even though I knew I had every reason to be mad at her, even though I knew that she wasn't right for me, I couldn't stop myself from missing her. She had barely been gone and yet it felt like a hole had opened up in my chest. I wondered if I would ever be able to get over her again. It had been difficult enough last time, and then we'd just had the one night together.

Then, I hadn't known that we had a kid together. Then, I hadn't known that our lives were inextricably linked, forever, for better or worse.

How could I love her so much when she clearly cared so little about me? How could I love her when the whole time, she had apparently had one foot out the door, ready to leave? Who knew how many hours she had spent poring over job opportunities, applying to various positions, sending out resumes, while I thought she was happily working on our joint project for Devin.

Was that what it had all been about? The reason she had been so desperate to get added to the project in the first place, the reason she had thrown everything she had into the job? Not because she wanted to do well here, but because she wanted to get closer to him? I felt stupid for not having realized that sooner.

I should have realized it. I should have expected it. Somehow, I had let myself believe that things were going well between us, that there was no way she was going to just disappear on me. I had been an idiot. I had basically handed her my heart and asked her to break it.

Only this time, it was going to hurt even more than it had last time. Fuck, I was such an idiot.

There was a knock on the door. Devin poked his head in, and immediately I felt my blood boil. There was a part of me that felt terrible about that. I should be glad he was getting such a conscientious worker for his company. If nothing else, he was my friend. Logic couldn't help me feel less terrible about things, though.

We were friends, all right. And friends didn't go around stealing their friends' best employees.

I knew that at the end of the day, though, it wasn't the job thing I was pissed about. So let her go work somewhere else. The part that really got to me was the fact that he was...

Well, I supposed I couldn't be mad at him for flirting with her. After all, he didn't know I had a thing for her. That I was sleeping with her—that we had Ronny. He didn't know any of that; I had been careful to keep it from him. For all he knew, she was single and unattached.

Somehow, that only made me angrier, even though it had been my decision to keep it all a secret.

I wondered if it would have made a difference if I had told him about things before. Maybe we would have lost the investment deal, but maybe I would have managed to hang on to Rian. Or else managed, at least, to not lose her to one of my good friends.

"Lunch?" Devin asked, quirking an eyebrow at me.

"Get the fuck out of my office," I found myself snapping, even though I knew it was about the least professional thing I could do.

Devin looked shocked. Rather than leave, he stepped into my office, shutting the door firmly behind him. "What the hell is wrong with you?" he asked. "You've been pissy ever since I came into town. Last I heard, we were on good terms —or did my investing a bunch of money in your company not help that?" He rolled his eyes sarcastically.

"Take the money back. I don't care," I said, throwing my hands in the air. "As far as I'm concerned, we have nothing more to do businesswise."

"And here I thought you were excited about this product line," Devin said, shaking his head. "Look, I don't know what the hell happened, but is this the way you normally do business? Because you're wasting my fucking time, man."

"Is this the way that *you* normally do business?" I retorted. "Sweep in and steal my best employees? Are you even interested in the product line at all, or was that just a ruse so you could determine which employees I couldn't stand to lose?"

"I don't know what you're talking about," Devin said, frowning. For a moment, he really didn't look like he had any idea.

I snarled wordlessly, brandishing the paper printout that

Beth had helpfully left on my desk, the one that had been taunting me since I came back after shouting at Rian in the parking lot. "I know Rian went asking you for a job. I'm sure you gave it to her, too, if her resignation earlier is anything to go by. Or if not you, then someone definitely gave her something!"

Devin's frown deepened. Slowly, he shook his head. "I never got any sort of email from her," he said, shrugging broadly and helplessly.

"Bullshit," I spat. "Take a look at this."

I tossed the paper toward him, letting it drift to the floor. I knew I was acting childishly, but I couldn't seem to help it. I hated the thought of never seeing Rian again, and I hated the thought of losing her to my friend even more so. She never would have met Devin if I hadn't brought her onto this project. I wished it weren't so easy to pick out all the ways he might be better for her.

Devin took two quick steps forward and snatched up the paper, his eyes scanning it. "This isn't real," he said firmly.

"What, you think I'm making it up?" I asked snidely.

"I didn't say that," Devin said mildly. "But I do think that *someone* is making something up. Or are you trying to tell me that Rian routinely misspells her name as 'Rain'? That smacks of an autocorrect error to me, but not one that someone would make with their name, especially not in an important email message where they're asking someone for a job because they have good attention to detail."

I frowned. "I don't know," I said. I wanted to let that doubt grow, to believe that of course Rian wouldn't have written that email. At the same time, I was afraid to trust her again. It had bitten me in the ass once before. I had been stupid to believe that this time might be any different. Of course she was going to leave again.

"This isn't even her phone number, is it?" Devin asked,

still peering at the email. "I thought all your numbers were 402 numbers. This is a 357 number."

I reluctantly got out of my seat and went over to look. I swore when I saw that he was right. That wasn't Rian's number at all. Not her work number, and not her cell phone either. I stomped over to my desk and called the number. Sure enough, some guy named Gary answered it.

"Wrong number," I muttered and hung up. I looked over at Devin. It was suddenly very quiet in my office.

"Where did this come from?" Devin finally asked.

I stared at him and then frowned, walking toward the door. "Beth, could you come in here for a moment?" I asked. Surely she wouldn't have done something like this... Except that I knew that she had. Suddenly, everything made so much sense.

Beth had been jealous and trying to cause a rift between Rian and me. She knew about the dinner. She must have realized I wasn't interested in her and decided that at the very least she could try to break me up and get a little revenge. Or free me up to get with her in the future. She had been the one to tell me that everyone was gossiping over Rian and Devin, and she had been the one to give me the email.

I felt sick as I realized I had ruined things with Rian over *this*.

When Beth came into my office, she initially looked happy. But then, she looked back and forth between me and Devin. Doubt appeared on her face, and she bit her lower lip. When I held up the email, she ducked her head.

"Look, I don't know if it's true or not," she muttered. "Rian just asked me to read over it and check if it sounded okay."

"I highly doubt she would ask you for that," I said. "She has her own assistant for that."

"Fine!" Beth snapped. "I made it up, okay?" She folded her arms across her chest. "So what, am I fired now or something? You know that if you fire me, I'm going to sue you for wrongful termination."

"On what grounds?" I asked, flabbergasted. I didn't think I had ever done anything that could count as wrongful termination.

Beth worked to come up with some sort of answer, but before she could, Devin stepped in. "If you do, I'll personally testify about the fact that you not only lied but fabricated evidence and tried to convince your boss to fire a good employee," he said. "Something tells me the judge might not be so willing to listen to you if you're a proven liar."

Beth's face darkened. I couldn't help but feel grateful to know that in spite of everything else, Devin was still on my side.

"Beth, you know I have to let you go," I said.

Her eyes turned stormy, but she seemed to know that she had lost. Without another word, she turned on her heel and walked out of there, slamming the door shut behind her.

I rubbed a hand wearily across my face. "Devin, I'm sorry," I said honestly. "I should have gotten all the facts."

Devin shrugged. "Don't worry about it," he said. He grinned crookedly. "So you and Rian?"

For a moment, I debated not telling him about her still. I remembered what it had felt like to think she was trying to get with him, though. If I said no, I was giving him all the entrance that he needed to flirt with her in the future. If that wasn't something that I wanted to witness, then I had to come clean to him. Whatever it might mean for my job and for the company.

Suddenly I realized that there were much more important things than my position with the company.

"Yeah," I said. "No one knows about it, but yeah."

Devin nodded. "I had a feeling something was up the other day. Glad you told me before I really made an ass of myself." He winked at me. "So I assume if you got that mad at me, you haven't talked to her about it yet?"

I groaned. "I confronted her," I admitted. "And when she tried to tell me that she hadn't done anything wrong, I basically told her that she was lying and that I never wanted to see her again."

Devin winced. "What are you going to do?" he asked.

"I think I have an idea," I said slowly.

I only hoped that Rian was willing to take me back. I knew I had fucked up royally, but I had an inkling of a plan that might make her realize how serious I was about her. I just hoped it would work.

CHAPTER 28

RIAN

There was a knock on the door. I knew I should probably get up and answer it. But what did it matter? I didn't care about who was on the other side of that door. Ronny was at school, and I had quit my job. That meant as far as I was concerned, unless Ronny's school called me, the rest of the world didn't need to exist.

I knew I needed to pull it together. Find a new job, move on, even if it meant moving out of Nebraska again. Ronny depended on me. I couldn't let things go to shit just because I was sad.

But I was damn sad, and I had basically been moping ever since things had gone bad with Wes. I couldn't help feeling bitter about the way things had gone down. Wes didn't trust me, and even though there was no reason he should, it still hurt.

I had let myself expect so much more this time. Last time, there hadn't been any expectations. Last time, it had just been a one-night thing, and even though it hurt, I told myself it was never meant to be a forever thing.

This time, I had let myself start to picture a future with

him. This time, I had actually thought that things might work out with Wes. He had given me every reason to believe he was over the way things had happened before, and that he wanted to be there in the future.

Somehow, it had all gone up in smoke. Somehow, I had lost him again, this time through no fault of my own. I kept thinking things over, wondering if there was any way I could have done things differently, if there was any way I could have shown him I truly never wanted to leave. That I wanted us to be a family, forever.

Still, knowing there was nothing I could have done differently didn't make things any better. Instead, I just felt hopeless. It made it hard to get out of bed in the mornings, even if I knew I had to hold things together for Ronny.

In part because even though I knew I couldn't have done anything differently this time, it didn't change the fact that I hadn't told him about Ronny years ago. I wasn't a liar about everything, but that was a huge thing to keep from him.

Somehow, I had thought that he might give me a second chance. Apparently not, though.

When I wasn't sad, I just felt angry. How dare he use the past against me like that. How dare he accuse me of lying about the other job. It would have been one thing if he had asked me if I had applied to other jobs. I would have told him straight up that he was an idiot to think that that was even a possibility.

Instead, he had yelled at me, convinced that I had not only applied for other jobs but chosen to accept one of them, without even having the guts to tell him. He had expected me, I guess, to just disappear in the middle of the night, to never let him see his daughter again. What the hell kind of a monster did he think I was?

I felt entirely out of sorts. Things had been starting to really feel good here. But now, all of that was over.

The knocking on the door became more insistent. For a moment, I snuggled deeper into my blankets. But suddenly, I faced a moment of panic. Did I even know where my cell phone was at the moment or if it was even charged? What if something had happened to Ronny and the school had tried to contact me but I hadn't gotten the message?

I was out of the bed in a flash. Whatever personal drama was going on in my life, it didn't give me any excuse to shirk my duties as a mother. I ought to be ashamed of myself.

I rushed to the door, still in my pajamas, and flung it open. For a moment, I could only stare at Wes standing there. There was a part of me that wanted to slam the door shut in his face. Who the hell did he think he was, just showing up here?

There was a bigger part of me, though, that ached just to see him standing there. I didn't know how I was ever going to trust him again either. I didn't know what he even wanted. At the same time, I had to hear what he was there to say. I had missed him more than I could ever have imagined.

Wes looked surprised to see me. I wondered if he had expected me to have already left, or if he was just surprised to see how haggard and worn-out I looked. I stared at him expectantly, not even sure what to say to him. If I opened my mouth first, I was probably going to say something that would make the situation worse. I had to hear what he wanted first.

I remembered that final threat, about how he would get lawyers involved if I wouldn't let him see Ronny. Was he here to serve me with the papers to sue me for custody? I felt like I might cry at the thought of that.

"We need to talk," he said quietly.

I stepped back to let him in. "Did you come here to make more accusations?" I couldn't help but ask.

Wes sighed and shook his head. "No, Rian. No." He

paused, looking uncertain and nervous. "I'm sorry," he said. "That email I thought that you had sent to Devin, it was all a lie. Beth faked it. I didn't realize it."

"I tried to tell you," I said.

"And I should have believed you," Wes said firmly. "I should have trusted you. I was just so scared I was going to lose you again."

Something about the raw note in his voice when he said that unlocked something in my chest. I grinned crookedly at him. He wasn't all forgiven, but I knew he wasn't the only one in the wrong here. "I guess," I said dryly, "that it might be harder to trust me because of the secret I kept."

Wes shook his head. "That's still no excuse for my actions," he said fervently. "It's not even the fact that I believed you might have gone behind my back to find this other job with Devin. Even after you told me you hadn't, though, I wouldn't listen to you. That's not the way relationships work. There has to be communication or of course things won't work out."

He cocked his head to the side, a slow smile spreading across his face. He still looked nervous, though. "That's why I lost you the first time, isn't it? Because we just jumped into bed with one another that night and never talked about what it might mean."

"And then after I found out I was pregnant, I didn't tell you about it," I added. "When you think about it, I guess most of our problems are from the fact that we don't talk about things very well."

I paused, wondering if this was the end of it. Just because we knew where our problems were, it didn't mean we could fix them. Or that he even wanted to fix things. What if he never trusted me again? I looked away from him.

"So what now?" I asked, hating how hollow my voice sounded. To be honest, I couldn't think of a single way to proceed from here. Things were wrecked between us, and just because we had talked about the argument we'd had, it didn't mean I suddenly had a job again. Could we put it all aside and build things again? Would they last any longer next time?

"I know you think I'm the one with one foot out the door, always ready to leave, but I'm afraid of that with you as well," I said, the truthful words spilling out of my lips before I had even paused to consider them. "I know that's probably not fair to you, because I'm the one who left before. I have to look out for Ronny, though. I hate the idea that I might let you into her life only for you to turn around and leave."

It would break Ronny's heart just as much as it would break mine. As it was, I hadn't told her yet about the fight Wes and I had had. She had asked about him a few times, and I had nearly gone to pieces. I hadn't known how to tell him that if she ever saw him again, it would be in a different capacity.

Because that would mean telling her he was her dad, and I didn't know how to do that on my own. What's more, I didn't want to do that on my own. It was another thing I had pictured doing with Wes right there by my side. A family kind of thing.

Something that we might never get, now. I couldn't help feeling depressed at the thought of everything I had lost.

"I'm in love with you," Wes said suddenly. I looked up at him in surprise. His grin was a little broader this time as he shrugged. "You know, in the spirit of better communication. I'm in love with you, and I want to build a family with you and Ronny."

I sighed, pessimism engulfing me as he mentioned Ronny. I couldn't help but circle back around to that threat he had made at the end of our fight the other day. Maybe he was just worried he would lose the custody battle since Ronny had been in my life for all these years while she barely knew him.

"You know I would never keep you from seeing Ronny, regardless of what happens between you and me," I said to him.

"I know that," Wes said honestly. I looked back at him, reading the truth there in his eyes. "I'm not just saying this because I want to see more of Ronny. I love you, Rian. I did back in college, too, although I didn't realize it until it was almost too late."

I stared at him. Still, I couldn't help but feel like things were somehow about to go to pieces again. "If you can't trust me not to cut and run, then you know there's no point to starting anything," I said unhappily. I wished I could just trust things, but I couldn't keep coming back around to this over and over again. It would kill me.

"Then let's give each other something to believe in," Wes said seriously. I stared at him as he dropped down on one knee. With a flourish, he pulled out a small box, opening it to reveal a small but elegant ring.

I stared at him, my hand creeping up over my mouth. Was he serious? I couldn't seem to ask; my lungs felt as though all the air had been punched out of them, in the best way possible.

"If you take this ring, I'm never letting you get away again," Wes said, still just as quietly serious. "Rian James, will you be mine—forever?"

"Yes," I heard myself whisper. My hand was shaking as Wes got to his feet and tenderly grasped my fingers, sliding the ring onto my third digit. He looked seriously in my eyes. I might have expected to feel some hesitation, or some nervousness at the very least.

Instead, this felt like the most right thing I had ever done, right up there with giving birth to Ronny.

I stared down at the ring on my finger, noting the way it glinted and sparkled in the light. "Wes, it's beautiful," I said, looking up at him, and I hoped he realized I meant more than just the ring itself. It was the promise of it all that was beautiful. We were going to make things work. Neither of us was ever leaving again, or else if we did, we would be leaving together. As a family.

I felt touched and overwhelmed. I felt shocked, but I also felt like this was somehow a long time coming. I remembered how good he had been with Ronny that first night he came over. I could picture years and years of nights like that, us together, a family. Yes, it was the perfect time for this.

Suddenly, I couldn't hold back. Maybe the whole trouble was that we had rushed into this thing too fast, or maybe it was the fact that after rushing into things too quickly, we had tried to slam on the brakes. I wasn't sure what it was that had made things so difficult before, but things felt right now. Things felt perfect, in fact.

I grabbed him, pulling him toward me, kissing him with everything I had. It was as though the past seven years' worth of feelings all came up at once, bubbling over into the kiss. It was messy, it was sweet, it was just this side of painful. It was everything I needed it to be. This, too, was perfect.

Equally perfect was the way my body fit against his and the way his fingers tangled in my hair. Equally perfect was the way he pushed against me as I started unbuttoning his shirt. There was no need to hold back, nothing to hide. No more secrets between us. And Ronny was at school. The whole house, the whole world, was ours for the next few hours.

We were naked in a flash, clothes forgotten on the floor. Wes laid me down on the sofa with a careful ease, looking deep into my eyes as he clambered on top of me. My legs fell open to him, inviting him to take me, to ravish me, to have every single inch of me.

As I grasped at the back of the couch, my ring twinkled again. Body and soul, I was his—forever.

I let him have me, chasing the blissful feeling of the two of us coming together in perfect synchronicity. At long last, we were on the same page, headed toward the same future. I wouldn't trade it for the world.

CHAPTER 29

WES

Making love to Rian felt like the release of all of my tensions that had been building up over the past few weeks. *She said yes.* I couldn't forget about that. Not with the sweet way she smiled up at me, and not with the way she seemed to be letting me in fully for the very first time. I reached out to twist my fingers with hers and could feel the ring there, a promise of what was to come. As if I needed more reassurance than the promise I could see in her eyes.

I knew we had the rest of our lives to explore one another, but I found myself wanting to know everything about her right now, starting with what made her squirm and what made her scream. I wanted to know every single thing I could do to her to get some sort of a response.

I wanted to know her inside and out, body and soul.

I started just kissing her, savoring the sweetness of her skin. I moved on to touching her, trailing my fingers across her curves, memorizing every little divot, every freckle, every line. As she wriggled with anticipation, I found myself smiling, kissing her gently. "Easy," I murmured. She gave a high-pitched whine in response, gone beyond words for the moment.

She wanted this badly. And I wanted it just as much.

When I finally delved into her depths—first with my fingers and then with my prick—I could feel her body working around me, squeezing out every inch of pleasure she could. She trembled and moaned, fingers clutching at me, legs restlessly flexing as pleasure shook her to the core.

I slowed down the rhythm, and she whimpered, tugging at me, urging me onward. I snapped my hips forward quickly, giving in to her pleas for a few moments before slowing down again. I grinned as her eyes flew open, and she glared at me.

"Wes, please," she said breathlessly.

And how could I deny her, when she looked like that?

I resumed my previous rhythm, groaning as she matched me movement for movement. We had always felt so in sync when we were having sex, but this time, things felt even more amazingly intimate and intense.

We had our whole futures spread out in front of us, and she was choosing to spend the rest of her life with me. I knew that things were bound to change, that no matter how beautiful and wonderful she was, no matter how in sync with one another we were, there were bound to be some challenges. But right then and there, the look in her eyes, the way she held onto me, the way that her soul matched up to mine, told me that no matter what those challenges were, we would find some way to get through them.

We came at the same time, crying out one another's names, shivering as we were engulfed by a powerful pleasure that was greater than any either of us had ever felt before. For one long and stunning moment, nothing existed in the world except for her, this amazing creature that I got to share my life with.

Slowly, the rest of it drifted back to me, starting with Ronny. *Our daughter.* I wasn't just going to get to spend the rest of my life with Rian. Even that would have been enough. Rian was everything I had ever wanted, after all, and now I knew she would be mine forever. But even better, she came with an adorable little girl whom I already couldn't wait to spend more time with.

I had never really been able to imagine myself with a family. I had never really known what I was looking for on that front. Or maybe it was just that I had been trying too hard not to look at Rian, in light of the fact that she had left me that once before.

Now, I was excited to share my life with her, but I was equally excited to become a dad. Or to find out I already was one, rather. I had never really realized that I wanted to have kids, but finding out that I had one, a daughter who was clever and sweet and everything I could have wished for? That was the icing on the cake.

Suddenly, though, Rian sighed in my arms. She didn't sound unhappy, but she didn't sound very content either. I felt cold dread seep into me. Maybe things were moving too quickly. It was something I had feared, when I'd first considered the idea of marrying her now. I knew I wanted this. But what would she think? Would she be able to trust me and to forgive me for not believing her when she said that she hadn't been looking for other jobs?

I still couldn't believe I had been ready to listen to Beth over her. That I had been willing to throw away the best thing in my life because of some office drama.

What if she didn't really want this? I could barely stand the thought of that.

"What now?" Rian asked quietly, her fingers tracing mine. When I looked down at her, she was carefully not looking at me, watching our hands rather than my eyes.

"What do you mean?" I asked, even though I had some inkling of what she was asking. Marrying her was in some ways simple. It was all the other things that would be tricky. Fortunately, I had some ideas about how to fix them. I just didn't want to overwhelm her too much with how much I had been thinking about this over the past few days.

Rian craned her neck so she could look up at me. "I don't have a job," she pointed out. "I don't know if Ronny and I are going to be able to stay."

"I want you back at the company," I said firmly. "What's more, Devin does as well. In fact, he isn't sure the board will still agree to the investment if you're not there to oversee things as the innovations manager. Which means that if you don't come back, there's a lot at stake."

I was playing dirty, sort of. I knew that. But at the same time, I really didn't want her to think she had to give her job up over us. She had worked too damned hard for too long. Besides, there was no way in hell I was letting her move away. Not her, and not Ronny either. I had to figure out some way to keep her here.

More than that, I wanted her to come back to work. To be honest, it had been kind of scary to show up that morning and find her still in her pajamas, with dark circles under her eyes and her whole persona looking dejected. It wasn't the way I pictured her at all. And it had been equally unsettling all week to come into the office and not have her presence there. I wanted to brainstorm with her. I wanted her opinion on seemingly every little thing.

"I can't come back, not if you and I are together," Rian said sadly. "I know how things work. You're technically my boss. Bad enough that we have a kid together, bad enough that we're sleeping together. But actually married? We couldn't do that. Everyone would suspect that any sort of raise I got, any sort of big work project I got, was just because I was sleeping with you. It wouldn't be right, and it would be fair to my career either."

"Of course not," I agreed, unable to keep from smiling. She hadn't said anything about not wanting the job. I had to assume that that was a good thing. "I already talked to George. He's agreed to be my supervisor. So from now on, you'll report directly to him for anything of importance like pay raises. In terms of the day-to-day operations, well, anyone who doesn't believe that you deserve the roles you take on certain projects, then they can just see if they could do better. But you and I both know they won't be able to."

Rian blinked, staring up at me. She slowly sat up. "How long have you been planning all of this?" she asked slowly. "You've already talked to George?"

For a moment, I wondered if I had said something wrong. I sat up as well. "Ever since you drove away, I knew that I made the biggest mistake of my life," I told her nervously. "If you don't feel the same way, then we can call this whole thing off. But I figured if we were even going to have a chance, I had to prove to you how serious I am about this. I don't want anything to get in the way of us being together. I want to be there for you and Ronny. That means figuring things out, not just rushing in head first like we've been doing. So I've spent the last few days trying to sort everything out."

Rian stared skeptically at me. "And George is really okay with this?" she asked, gesturing between us.

I laughed. "He didn't have much of a choice," I told her. "I told him that if he didn't accept this and help me find some way to make it work, then I would resign. He couldn't do without a CEO and an innovations manager. Not to mention what would happen with the deal with Devin's firm if neither of us were there."

Rian's eyes widened. "What would you have done if he had called your bluff?" she asked worriedly.

"There was no bluff," I said seriously.

"You couldn't possibly have meant that you would quit your job if you and I couldn't be together," Rian said, shaking her head.

I took both of her hands in mine, looking deep into her eyes. Once, I would have been hurt at the fact that she seemed so loath to accept that I was in it for good. But now, I realized she was just nervous. I set about dispelling that nervousness once and for all.

"Rian, you're worth more to me than any career could ever be," I said. "I can't wait to spend the rest of my life with you and Ronny. I mean it."

Rian's eyes shone with unshed tears, and she leaned in to kiss me again, even more fervently than the last time. When she finally pulled back, we were both breathless, and I could feel my body stirring with interest again.

"I love you," Rian said softly. "More than you'll ever know."

I grinned at her. "I thought we had talked about communication," I teased. "You're going to have to find some way to make sure I know."

Rian's eyes widened for a moment, and then her hand came to land on my member. "I think I can think of some way," she joked, smirking at me.

"Prove it," I said, smirking right back.

EPILOGUE

RIAN - ONE YEAR LATER

I couldn't help but feel nervous as I peeked into the ballroom. It was packed in there, people in every seat. I knew that Devin was expecting a good turnout, but this exceeded all of our expectations. I couldn't believe that in less than an hour, I was going to get up on a stage in front of all those people and try to run through the information about the new product line we were launching. Already, I couldn't seem to remember my own name, let alone what I was meant to say.

Two hands caught me by the waist, pulling me closer. "Don't tell me you're starting to second-guess this," Wes murmured in my ear, his suit-clad body fitting snugly against mine.

I covered his hands with my own. "This?" I retorted. "Never."

I smiled as I turned around in his arms, wrapping my arms around his neck. "It can't be the fanciness, because you look incredible," Wes said. "So what is it?"

I grinned sheepishly at him. "I don't think I've ever had to talk in front of this many people before, that's all."

"It's a pretty big crowd," Wes agreed seriously. "The Rian James I knew in college would never have gotten stage fright, though."

"The Rian James you knew in college was a very different person than who I am now," I said tartly, as though he didn't know that.

Wes laughed. "I'll be right there next to you the whole time," he promised me. "I'm sure Ronny will be as well."

I frowned. "Devin said he would keep an eye on her," I reminded him.

Wes snorted. "Let's just say, I think Devin's idea of keeping an eye on her might not be the same as your idea," he said. "Trust me, you don't want to know what she looked like the last time he dropped her off, while you were in New York for your friend's wedding and I had that group of investors from Chicago in for the weekend."

I groaned. "As though I needed one more thing to worry about tonight," I complained.

Wes grinned unrepentantly. "Just think: the more you worry about Ronny, the less capacity you have to worry about how many people are in that room."

I shook my head. "Well, I guess it's go time," I said, as I heard myself being introduced.

"Let's go, then," Wes agreed. He grabbed my hand for one last moment before we walked into the room amidst dazzling applause.

Things didn't go as terribly as I'd feared they might while we were on stage. Sure, there was that moment where Ronny came rushing over to us, having somehow made her way up the steps while Devin just shrugged from the sidelines. But she behaved herself once she was there, holding Wes's hand and beaming out at everyone, waving occasionally as people smiled and waved at her.

Afterward, Wes and I mingled with the crowd. Mike

Maglione came up to me almost the instant that Wes stepped away from my side, and I couldn't help but wince internally. I was pretty sure we were long past the days of Wes chewing off anyone's head who even so much as looked at me, but I knew that he wouldn't be too thrilled to see me talking to SugarPop's hottest young bachelor of the year.

Especially not as Mike handed me his business card. "For someone as young as you, you're doing an amazing job," he said. "And I don't mean that the wrong way! Obviously I'm young as well."

I smiled at him, deciding he was harmless. He wasn't the first person to offer me a new job since this whole thing with Devin's company had taken off. "Thanks, Mike," I said, taking the card and slipping it into my pocketbook. "But I'm perfectly happy where I am at the moment. More than, in fact."

Mike shook his head. "I was afraid you might say that," he said ruefully.

Wes slid an arm around my waist just then, handing me a glass of sparkling water. "Maglione, are you trying to steal away one of my best assets?" he asked jokingly.

Mike laughed. "Only because I could tell it wouldn't work," he said. "But it was worth a shot, wasn't it?"

He and Wes chatted for a minute, while I leaned into my husband's warmth. Afterward, he gave me a concerned look. "Do you need anything else?" he asked. "How are you feeling anyway? If you're tired, we can get out of here a little early. I already warned Devin that we might."

I laughed, unable to help it. He sounded so concerned, but I was just fine. "I've never met a more attentive man during a pregnancy," I said, smiling happily. I was the luckiest girl in the world, and I knew it.

It wasn't long after we had gotten married that I found out that I was pregnant with our second child. I hadn't really been trying to get pregnant, per se, although we had definitely talked about the possibility of giving Ronny a younger brother or sister. Now, everything seemed to be falling into place. With this product launch, I was due to take a little time off. And Wes had been everything I could have wished for and then some.

He seemed to be trying to make up for lost time, or for not being there during the first pregnancy. He was practically waiting on me hand and foot, and anytime I did anything that he considered to be too dangerous, he was there to gently remind me to look out for myself and for the baby.

That very morning, in fact, he had told me that he wished that he could carry me everywhere because he was so afraid that I might fall and injure myself and the baby. I had to remind him that I had been fine in the first pregnancy and that we James women were strong and independent. At the same time, I secretly liked how overboard he was going. I found it ridiculously endearing, and it was reassuring to know that he wanted to be there for this youngster, just as much as he had shown that he wanted to be there for me and Ronny.

He was going to be a great father. Again.

I was just happy to know that I had his support through this pregnancy. I could have done it on my own again, but at the same time, it was nice to have him there with me, by my side.

A photographer came up to us suddenly. "Would the two of you mind if I took a picture of you?" he asked.

I glanced over at Wes, shrugging. There had been a time when we had first been engaged that I had been more nervous about things like this. I didn't know how much was all right for people to know. After all, anyone from the outside might think that Wes was still my boss. Even if not, they might think our relationship as colleagues and also spouses was inappropriate.

Those days were behind us now, though. Everyone who we did business with knew about our relationship, and to be honest, I think most of them appreciated the fact that we were together. Wes and I were nearly always on the same page, and we were always good to brainstorm and bounce ideas off one another, meaning that any pitch we gave was all the stronger, the result of both of our creativity and talents.

"Sure," Wes said to the photographer. But before the man could take his photo, however, Wes reached over and caught Ronny as she zoomed past, lifting her shrieking with giggles up into the air. He put her on his shoulders and then turned and wrapped an arm around me. "Better get the whole family, though," he said, winking.

The photographer grinned and held up his camera. There was a flash, and then Ronny wiggled around, trying to be let down. Wes hung her upside down by her ankles for a moment, and there was another laugh. The photographer smiled at me. "Don't worry, I won't use that one. But you might want it for the memories? I'll send it to you."

"Thank you," I said, smiling warmly at him. Soon, there would be pictures of our family all over our house, I imagined. The three of us, soon to become the four of us. Wes and I had lain awake for hours some nights, just talking about how perfect things were for us. They were only getting better, too.

I had an amazing partner. He was kind and he was caring, and he loved our daughter as though he'd been there for her whole life. At work, we were raising the bar together, both of us working hard and putting out the best that we could.

At the end of the day, I got to come home to kisses and back rubs and a man who was just as willing to pitch in with the dishes as he was to help me cook. We were the perfect team, both professionally and at home.

"Mom, Devin said we can go for ice cream after the party because they don't have any here," Ronny suddenly announced.

I groaned. "I'm going to kill him," I said. Devin was wonderful with Ronny, almost like the uncle she had never had, but he sure had a tendency to spoil her. I had a feeling the same would hold true for this new little one, if the number of baby gifts he had already given us were anything to go by.

"I couldn't help it—think of how adorable it'll look on him. Or her," he said every time.

Speak of the devil, Devin appeared just then, holding his hands in the air. "I said that if you agreed, we could go for ice cream." He leaned in closer. "Besides, I figured you two might want a little time to decompress after all of this. I don't mind taking her for an hour or two."

I shook my head. "You've already watched her for half of the night," I protested. I didn't want to impose on him, even though I knew he loved her, and even though he kept offering.

Devin shrugged. "I don't mind—seriously," he said. "Besides, this night is about you guys. This is huge. You deserve a little time to celebrate."

"This night is about you, too," Wes reminded him. "We couldn't have done all of this without your investment."

Devin grinned. "Then I guess it's all about your wife," he teased. "I was about to quit entertaining your ideas about the project after you took me fishing that one day. You're just lucky that you thought to invite this one out to brunch with us, or things could have turned out very differently for all of us."

I burst out laughing, while Wes sputtered with indignation. I gave him a little nudge. "Told you that you needed to add me on to that project," I said, grinning at him.

Wes shook his head. "I guess I've always known that I needed you," he said gravely, putting an arm around my shoulders again. Heat smoldered in his eyes as he looked down at me.

I turned back to Devin, smiling sheepishly. "I guess a little ice cream wouldn't hurt," I said, making the executive decision. It was something we had struggled with some when we had first gotten engaged: I had gotten so used to calling all the shots when it came to Ronny's life that I forgot that he would have his opinions, too. We had figured out a way to make things work, though.

Now, though, Wes squeezed my shoulder in agreement.

Devin chuckled. "You got it," he said, while Ronny cheered and danced in circles around us. I didn't know if she was ever going to get to bed that night after all of the excitement and the addition of sugar. But then again, as I looked back at Wes, I knew that the only reason I was going to get to sleep that night was because of the exhaustion that pregnancy brought on.

Sex would be nice, but I had a feeling that night, Wes would try to outdo himself in terms of taking care of me. But a massage sounded pretty nice after being on my feet all day. I would get him back for all of this at some point, of course.

We had the rest of our lives to show one another how much we truly cared for each other. We were going to be all right.

I felt a flush of contentedness rush through me. I couldn't be luckier. I had the perfect daughter, the perfect husband, the perfect job, the perfect life.

Once upon a time, I had been so worried about how things might turn out if I opened myself up and let Wes into my life. Things had turned out better than I could ever have dreamed of, though.

We walked out of there arm in arm that night. The party was far from over, but I was tired. Besides, I didn't need to be there. All the congratulations I needed were there in my husband's pride for what we had accomplished together. And the last thing I needed was another job offer. I had everything I wanted already, right here beside me.

And growing inside of me, I thought, my hand resting on my belly as I got into the car.

Wes smiled over at me as he buckled his own seat belt. I had a feeling he was thinking exactly the same thing. It might have taken us some time to get on the same page, but we were certainly there now.

"Let's go home," Wes said quietly, putting the keys in the ignition.

"Yes," I agreed, "let's go home." It had been surprisingly easy to find a home in a townhouse in Nebraska. The place already felt more like home, after just a year there, than my place in New York ever had. But then again, anywhere would be home with Wes and Ronny by my side.

The End

Made in the USA
Monee, IL
12 January 2020